# DUMPSTER FIRE

LIFE SUCKS #3

ELISE FABER

DUMPSTER FIRE
by Elise Faber

DUMPSTER FIRE
Copyright © 2021 ELISE FABER
Print ISBN: 978-1-946140-88-3
eBook ISBN: 978-1-946140-87-6
Cover Art by Jena Brignola

# LIFE SUCKS SERIES

# ONE

## DUMPSTER FIRE

Rob

IT WAS PROBABLY a morbid birthday tradition for him to be sitting in a graveyard, a beer at his hip, a bouquet of daisies laid across his late wife's headstone.

But . . . the daisies had been her favorite.

Well, the beer had been her favorite, too.

His best friend, his buddy, his *love*. Carmella had watched more sports than him, had gotten him turned on to IPAs, had dished shit his way more than anyone else. And . . . he'd loved her more than anything.

But now she was gone, and he was sitting in the graveyard on his birthday because it was something to do when his life was filled with absolutely nothing.

Cool.

*Super positive outlook you have there.*

The mental voice was Carmella's, and it was no surprise she was giving him shit from the other side of the grave.

He just wished she was around to give it in person.

That wasn't to be, of course.

And Rob knew it was time he stopped grieving. Or if not that, then it was time he stopped hanging around the graveyard. Because he'd had enough beers to admit that he'd spent more than just his birthday night here.

He'd spent *too* many nights here.

*Stop moping, Rob. Chin up and carry on.*

But he didn't want to put his chin up and carry on. He wanted things to go back to normal. He wanted . . . Carmella.

Sighing, he collected his empties and stood, slightly wavering because the bottles numbered six, and that was four more than he normally indulged in graveside. Which meant he had a couple of stumbling feet and a pair of eyes that weren't tracking exactly right. Not that his drunkenness was a big deal. He lived in Stoneybrook, and Stoney put the brook into small ass towns.

*And that makes absolutely no sense, babe,* Carmella told him. *Time to go home and sleep it off.*

Since he didn't argue with his wife—or at least didn't argue and expect to win—Rob turned in the direction of his house, which was all of two blocks away.

See? Small town.

Two blocks to the graveyard. Two on the other side to downtown. Three, max, to the beach he didn't go to any longer—or at least not very often. He'd learned to stomach a lot of things in the two years since Carmella had passed, but he had a hell of a time stomaching going *there*. Especially alone.

He just couldn't.

*Go, babe.*

Nodding in response to the voice he knew was definitely not real, Rob weaved his way through the graves, dumped the bottles in the trash can near the exit—never let it be said that he wasn't a neat drunk—and started walking along the road that would lead home.

It was dark, nearing midnight, with only the moon to light his way.

But again, that was okay. Because Stoneybrook was small and had no traffic *and* because he'd done this walk more times than he could count.

He could probably do it with his eyes closed.

The town was absolutely still and quiet, having rolled up its streets many hours before.

So, the last thing Rob expected to see was a car.

He'd just stepped out of the shadows across the road from his house when he saw the headlights . . . coming right toward him.

He should have moved.

Instead, he froze.

This was it. *This* was when his loneliness would end, when he would finally see Carmella again. *Finally.*

He closed his eyes, sucked in a deep breath, and waited.

Tires on the road, a roaring noise closing in, a horn blaring.

And . . .

The car screeched to a halt.

Inches from him. Close enough he could feel the heat of the engine, hear the ticking of the metal parts inside the transmission.

Disappointment flooded through him, his eyes flying open.

Then the door shot open, and his gaze flew there just in time to see heels appear on the street. High, *high* heels the likes of which Carmella would never wear. They were followed by bare ankles, calves, and knees, and then a glimpse of thigh encased in a short, tight skirt. Another thing Carmella would never wear.

"What in the fuck do you think you're doing crossing the street without looking in the middle of the night?" the woman yelled.

*That* was Carmella.

Fierce. Tough.

But this wasn't *his* Carmella. Rob wobbled slightly, his stomach churning, the beers catching up with him all at once, even as he had the distinct thought that this woman was. Not. His. Carmella.

"It's my birthday," he muttered.

"I don't give a fuck if it's the pope's birthday—" She broke off.

Probably because right then he bent at the waist and puked all over his own shoes.

He couldn't even summon up the strength to be embarrassed . . . because the moment after his stomach was emptied, the whole world went black.

The last thing he heard was,

"Shit. Motherfucker. Son of a bitch!"

And that made him smile.

Because *that* mouth was his Carmella.

# TWO

## DEAD BODIES WERE HEAVIER THAN THEY APPEARED

Soph

SHE STARED AT THE ROAD, well, at the man who'd just collapsed in a puddle of his own vomit, and tried to figure out what to do.

She'd come to this small town to get away from the attention that had become unbearable after her latest film, starring alongside *the* Finn Stoneman—Hollywood's most popular leading man—had broken box office records. She was the *Next Hot Thing*, and that wasn't ego talking. Her publicist had told her that exact title had graced the cover of no less than five magazines.

The chance of a lifetime.

The success she'd dreamed of for ten years as a working actress in Los Angeles.

Now it was here, and she'd be an idiot to not be thrilled.

But . . . she was an idiot because she *wasn't* thrilled.

Instead, it all felt empty and meaningless. The endless press and soundbites and outfits—always a different one, because—gasp—she couldn't wear the same thing twice. Oh, the horror!

She still loved acting, still felt incredibly lucky to have gotten her big break.

It just . . . wasn't as wonderful as she'd always dreamed it might be.

There. She said it.

Soph was a poor, not-quite-rich-but-at-least-had-some-savings girl, who had her face plastered on magazines and social media and had discovered that the green grass on the other side wasn't always so green.

Fun times.

None of which had anything to do with the passed-out man she was staring at in the center of the road.

She'd nearly hit him, the streetlights overhead only doing so much to illuminate his earlier emergence from the shadows. And that had been when he was moving. Now he might as well be a speed bump in the middle of the road.

After reaching into the car to hit the button for her hazard lights, she moved over to the man, wrinkling her nose at the not-so-pleasant odor.

Beer.

Pizza.

Ugh. Seriously the worst combination ever.

Years of bartending in between acting gigs had taught her that much.

"Hey!" she said, loud and abrupt, nudging him with the toe of her heel. "Wake up!"

He groaned, shifted slightly, but didn't open his eyes.

"You're in the road, dumbass," she barked. Yes, it was rude, but he *was* in the road and if a little rudeness got him up and moving so he didn't get run over, then she'd dish out what she needed to.

Unfortunately, her cajoling had limited effect.

He continued to lie prone on the street.

"Fuck," she muttered and kicked off her heels. Then stepped behind him, looped her arms beneath his, and heaved.

And made it all of six inches because he was a heavy fucker.

This was what moving a dead body would be like, she supposed, knowing that she would be a shit serial killer, if she were so inclined, not even being able to move a body.

But she was stubborn, and she was strong—thanks to Pilates six days a week—and so after a plentiful amount of heaving, cursing, and groaning, she finally managed to drag his ass to the sidewalk.

She probably shouldn't have risked moving him, she thought as she slipped out of her coat and bundled it under his head. He might have an injury she couldn't see. But he hadn't fallen very far, just bent in half and puked then sort of crumbled slowly to the ground.

Certainly, the road had been the bigger danger.

She didn't think he'd even have a bruise in the morning.

In the meantime, she would have a smarting foot, she realized as she sat next to him, lifting said foot and seeing that she'd sliced the bottom of it on something in the road.

Sighing and knowing there was no hope for it, she hobbled her way back to her car, dug around in her purse for her cell, then her suitcase for a hoodie, her tiny first aid kit, a pair of socks, her sneakers, and her cozy, stupidly expensive blanket she used for long haul flights.

The latter she'd sacrifice to the idiot on the sidewalk, the former she slipped over her head, and the middle three were for her feet.

She hobbled back over to the man in question, tucked the blanket around him and sat down, stealing a corner for herself so she didn't flash who knew what was in the road or surrounding shadows as she tended to her foot. But before commencing her ministrations, she dialed Finn's number and put him on speaker.

It rang a few times before he picked up.

"Soph?" he asked. "Did you land?"

"Yeah. I'm here."

"What's the matter?" His tone was concerned, and she was reminded that the man wasn't only a talented actor, but he was a skilled director as well, able to coax the smallest emotions from his cast.

"I've got a problem."

"What is it?"

She sighed then explained what happened.

"Shit," he muttered when she'd finished. "You're not hurt?"

"No," she said. "I'm fine. *He's* fine, too, I think. Just passed out."

"Okay, good. Where are you exactly?"

"I'll send you a pin." Thank God for technology and it enabling her to send him her exact location with only a few taps of her screen.

"Good," he said, and she heard him moving around in the background. "I'll be there in less than ten."

"Ten?" she asked. "You haven't even seen the pin yet."

He laughed. "This is Stoneybrook. Nothing is more than ten minutes away. I'll see you in a few, okay?"

"Okay." But she didn't hang up.

She had this feeling, one deep inside her gut telling her that something about her life had just changed.

Finn must have sensed her disquiet. "You want me to stay on the line with you?"

Soph shook herself. "No, of course not." She released a breath. "I'm just tired. I'll see you in ten." Then she hung up before he could say anything further, quickly pulling up the maps app and texting him a pin marking her location.

Two minutes later, she'd cleaned the cut—well, it was more abrasion than cut—and slapped a couple of bandages on her foot. That finished, she was just tugging on her socks when headlights appeared in the distance and was shoving her feet into her sneakers, the hurt one protesting mightily, as the car pulled up beside hers, Finn's head poking out the window.

"I see you've gotten the Stoneybrook welcome."

She frowned. "I thought you told me this was a nice, quiet town."

He grinned, put the car into park, and left it running, right there in the middle of the road.

Which was probably a perfectly safe spot, considering she hadn't seen hide nor hair of another car or person in the time she'd been sitting there—not that it had been long. But the truth was that it was strangely quiet, the light breeze from the ocean rustling the trees, but everything else was still and peaceful and . . . so damned quiet it was almost unnerving.

"Who'd you hit?" he asked, coming over to her.

She narrowed her eyes. "I told you, I didn't hit anyone."

"Rob!"

Soph blinked, realized she'd missed seeing Finn's wife, Shannon, getting out of the car. She ran over to where they sat on the sidewalk, her eyes concerned as they met Sophie's. "You okay?"

"I'm fine," she said. "And he's fine, too. Just drunk and passed out, and *not* hit by my car," she added, glaring up at Finn.

Shannon wrinkled her nose. "He needs a shower."

Soph nodded. "And to burn these clothes. They've got puke and road juice all over them."

"Road juice?" Finn asked.

She shuddered. "Poor choice of words," she said apologetically, to which Shannon and Finn both smiled and shrugged.

"His name is Rob?" Soph asked. "Do you know where he lives, so we can get him home?"

"Yup," Finn said and bent. "You sure he didn't hit his head?"

She nodded.

"Good." He thrust one arm under Rob's shoulders, the other under his knees, and hefted him up in a move that belied Finn's strength because, as Soph personally knew, Rob was *heavy*. Then without preamble, Finn proceeded to carry Rob up the driveway of the house she'd stopped in front of. "Can you grab the key, sweetheart?"

Shannon had been folding Sophie's blanket and jacket, and she quickly passed them over, following her husband up the drive.

Soph probably should have left then, but instead, she trailed Finn and Shann, watching as the latter lifted a planter on the porch, retrieved a key, and then let them into Rob's house.

And Soph probably should have left *then*.

But she didn't, just followed them into the house.

It was small and cozy, with wide windows and a woman's touch evident in the throw pillows on the couch, the smattering of blankets on the back cushions, the knickknacks and flowers on the table in the hall, the tiny sign declaring, *It's Good to be Home* with keys hanging from hooks on the bottom of it.

She let her gaze slide around the open space, obliquely aware of Finn moving up the stairs, of the noise of a shower turning on, even as she kept studying the rooms as though they were the most interesting museum exhibit she'd ever seen.

Smooth granite counters in a light color she couldn't discern in the dimness, cabinets that were also an indeterminate shade— were they white or gray or perhaps a pale, pale yellow? A large sink, a full-sized fridge, a microwave mounted over a stove. And there was a tea kettle, shining bright silver as though the moonlight were shining directly through the window behind that large sink simply to highlight it in its rays.

And she was drawn to that kettle like a beacon.

She padded across the room, saw that it was inscribed with words, but when she bent close to read them, they were the absolute last thing she expected to see there.

Which was incongruous, she knew, because how could she possibly know what was engraved on that silver metal? She'd never been in this house, never met this man, never—

*Real men drink tea.*

That was it.

So was it a joke between him and his wife or girlfriend? Because clearly, the man wasn't single. She hadn't needed to be in this home for longer than two minutes to recognize that—and yes, she knew that was a slightly sexist statement or at least thought, because she was implying only women decorated homes. But it wasn't that at all. She knew plenty of men back in Hollywood who could design the hell out of their houses—and do it a hell of a lot nicer than she could. It was just . . . there was something about a woman's touch that made a home feel . . . *cozier*, she supposed.

Like a family was apt to hop out at any moment.

Or maybe that was just what she'd always hoped to find.

Wishful thinking when her own family had been—

"Thank you for helping him," Shan said.

Sophie jumped and spun around, heart pounding like she'd intruded on something she shouldn't have because . . . well, she supposed she *had* intruded. On this man's house. On his life.

"It's just lucky I didn't hit him," she murmured.

Shan sighed and nodded. "He *is* lucky," she said. "He just doesn't know it."

"What do you mean?"

"He—" A shake of her head. "I shouldn't say anything."

"It's okay," Soph told her. "You don't have to tell me anything." She took a step to the door. "But I probably should head out, wouldn't want his wife or girlfriend to find a strange person in their house."

Shan made a strangled noise.

"What is it?" she asked.

The curvy brunette winced. "I know I shouldn't be telling you this, especially since I hate everything to do with gossip." She bit her lip. "But Stoneybrook is a small town, and this is common knowledge, and I would hate for you to stumble upon something or *say* something—"

"Say *what?*" Sophie asked.

"Rob is widowed. Has been for a couple of years now."

Sophie's heart froze. "Oh shit," she whispered. He was young, in the full bloom of life, and to lose someone at that point in their marriage must have been brutal. "That—I—how?" she whispered.

"Car accident," Shan said.

"Shit."

"Yeah," Shannon agreed. "And today is his birthday. And the anniversary of her death."

She'd known the first, thanks to his proclamation. The second, well . . . "*Shit.*"

"Yeah."

Sophie sighed. "Poor guy must have really loved her."

Shan nodded, her vibrant blue eyes bright. "They were inseparable from kindergarten. He used to tell me he remembered the day Carmella walked into the classroom with purple overalls, a tiny Patriots jersey, and mischief in her eyes, and he knew then that he was going to spend the rest of his life with her."

Eyes stinging, Soph swallowed several times before she could answer. "That's lovely."

"It really is."

"And sad."

"That, too."

Silence.

Long enough that Soph started getting an itchy feeling in her spine, one telling her that she had way overstepped and should go. No. Like she should *really* go. Like right this instant.

Like ten minutes ago.

Like before she'd come into this house and intruded on his pain.

"I should go," she blurted.

Shannon nodded. "I'm sure you're tired after your flight."

Soph began inching toward the door, that itchy feeling growing when her eyes alighted on all the female touches, on the remnants of what once must have been a very lovely life.

"Yes, I am."

Then she ran.

# THREE

# MISERABLE: JUST THE WAY HE LIKED IT

Rob

HE WOKE up naked and unhappy.

Naked because he'd woken up halfway through the cold shower Finn had tossed him into, suddenly sober enough to curse and wriggle his way out of his wet clothes, but not sober enough to manage more than a quick cleanup, followed by stumbling to his bed.

Unhappy because the light pouring through the window was a jagged dagger jabbing through his eyes and stabbing repeatedly at his brain.

Fun times.

Groaning, he rolled over and squinted at the clock, seeing it was nearly noon.

Fucking hell, he was late for work.

Four fucking hours late for work.

Yanking at the still-damp towel he'd wrapped around his waist during his stumbling trek to bed, he managed to extract himself and sit up after copious amounts of cursing and wrestling.

Okay, more cursing than wrestling.

Either way, at the end of it, he was sitting up, his head throbbing, and his eyes alighting on the tablets of ibuprofen, the cup of water, and the note, his name written on the front in a sleek feminine script.

And that was when he remembered the woman.

Not just Finn.

But a woman in high, *high* heels and a tight, purple skirt. Skin turned silver in the moonlight, shapely thighs, an ass that had been in love with all that snug fabric. Or maybe *he'd* been in love with it.

Either that, or he'd enjoyed the cursing. Because she had a mouth on her like a soldier, and . . .

He frowned, rubbing his temple.

Then remembered some more.

"Fuck," he groaned, the image of the car screeching to a halt inches from him, the door opening, the goddess emerging, and then him.

His vision going blurry.

His stomach churning.

And him puking on himself.

Then . . . blackness, the world fading away until that cold shower, until Finn had hauled him into a semi-sober state. Which meant that his friend had either stumbled upon him in that street, in the puddle of vomit, or the mystery woman somehow knew Finn and had called him for help.

Because she *was* a mystery woman.

He knew everyone in this small town, and everyone knew him, knew his story, knew why he'd ended up such a fucking mess the night before.

But not her.

She hadn't looked at him with pity. Nope, she'd glared at

him, fury etched into the lines of her face, making her dark eyes spark in the moonlight. What he wouldn't give to see them in the sunlight, to discern their true color—deep brown or light or maybe hazel or a dark green or blue.

They would be beautiful; he knew that in his gut.

Just as he somehow knew that the cursing she'd unleashed on him was merely a teaser, that she had a whole repertoire at her disposal, and she wouldn't be afraid to use it.

How?

He couldn't begin to explain it except to say that it was a feeling laced right into the very fabric of his being.

And *that* was enough nonsense before he even made it fully out of bed.

He reached for the note and unfolded it, disappointment flowing through him.

*Rob,*

*I called in sick for you. The Fosters say their job will hold until tomorrow.*

*-Shan*

Happy.

He knew he should be happy that Shannon was a good enough friend to have called the couple whose home he was remodeling, to have explained why he hadn't shown—though hopefully she'd not given them the he's-drunk-out-of-his-mind-and-an-absolute-mess excuse. Though they probably knew anyway. Just as the whole town would know why he hadn't been able to cope yesterday, why they'd all looked at him with pity.

His birthday.

The anniversary of his wife's death.

And now, he was thirty.

He and Carmella had planned on being in the Caribbean

with warm surf beneath their toes, rather than the cold beach-front they'd grown up with. But now, she was in the ground and he was alone, and he was too much of a fucking mess to even think about moving on.

Plus, even when he'd tried going on a few dates when the loneliness got to be too much, they hadn't gone well. He was barely human these days and certainly a long way from being charming. And funny story, women usually preferred when the man they were seeing wasn't still hung up on someone from his past.

They also preferred for said man to not drunkenly wander into the street, nearly get themselves run over, and they certainly preferred their man to not puke on their own shoes after said events.

But he'd still hoped that the note had been from *her*.

Ridiculous, he knew.

But he'd made it a fucking skill, his ability to hope for things to be different, to wish they could change, to think and dream about all the ways his life might be different if he'd not lost Carmella.

*You can't live with your head in the clouds, my love.*

He knew that. *God,* how Rob knew that.

And yet, it was so fucking difficult to live without *her*. He didn't have big dreams. He never had. A family, a house of their own, a quiet life, and Carmella. The girl he'd fallen for when he'd been all of six years old.

She'd been a whirlwind, a bundle of energy, outgoing and courageous and constantly pulling him out of his shell.

*But now I'm gone.*

Sighing, he stared at the picture on his nightstand, the distressed white wooden frame holding the photo of them on their wedding day.

She'd worn a lilac dress, had roses braided into her hair.

And he'd . . . fallen even more in love with her, until his heart beat only for her, until she been in the marrow of his bones.

*But now, I'm gone,* she repeated.

"Yes," he murmured, picking up the pills and swallowing them before chugging down the glass of water. "Yes, you are," he said, setting the cup down and moving into the bathroom that was practically a shrine to her. But of course it was—even without her products still on the counter, stowed in the shower, the cabinets, the drawers, each exactly where she'd left them—because he'd designed it for her.

Had found the hand-painted tile during their honeymoon and had paid an arm and a leg to have it shipped back to Stoneybrook.

Then had cursed his way through laying the hexagonal-shaped pieces, in mimicking the beautiful patterns they'd seen in the buildings of Morocco.

Memories, he knew, stroking a finger over the handle of her hairbrush.

In every inch of this house.

Comfort. It was supposed to be comfortable, that protective blanket he tugged around himself, but it wasn't feeling nearly as cozy. No, instead, it was starting to feel stifling, constrictive, and—

Guilt.

Because he shouldn't feel that way about his wife.

He should love and cherish the memories, not—

*Make a fucking shrine to me, my love.*

Rob sighed and sank down on the edge of the tub. "Yes, that," he whispered, knowing full well he was talking to an apparition in his mind. "But what the fuck am I supposed to do?" he muttered, head in his hands. "How do I make plans and live a life when we had ours all planned out together?"

Carmella didn't have an answer to that.

Which meant, neither did he.

---

LATER THAT NIGHT, he found himself on his front porch, a cup of tea in his hand and knowing that he needed to bite the bullet and either call Finn and Shannon to thank them for helping his sorry ass, or he needed to go see them and thank them in person.

They lived on the beach.

So he knew it would need to be a phone call.

"Weak, Hansen," he muttered, knowing that was true.

But he still pulled out his cell and called Finn anyway. Somehow, it wasn't strange to be on a first-name basis with the mega movie star, maybe because he'd met Finn through their mutual friend Pepper. Pepper O'Brien came from Hollywood royalty, but she was about as far from L.A. as they came. He'd actually gone on his first date after Carmella with the sweet, klutzy redhead, and while they'd not even gotten through their first round of drinks before Rob had been ousted by Pepper's now-husband, Derek, they had become friends.

And gotten closer when she'd stayed in town.

Then over the summer, she'd introduced him to Finn (he'd already known Shannon because . . . small town), but Rob had really enjoyed spending time with the couple and Shan's energic daughter, Rylie.

He'd become the fourth wheel, even occasionally letting himself be coaxed into beach time with Rylie, who truly was an unstoppable force, and could get him to move past the painful memory of his late wife to go build sandcastles with her on very rare occasions. It was always easier with the tiny first-grader, her unrelenting energy reminding him of Carmella—and certainly her mischief-making skills would have equaled, and perhaps topped, his wife's numerous troublemaking abilities.

The phone rang and went to voicemail, and Rob cursed, knowing he should do things the Stoneybrook way, with a six-pack of beer—none for him, since clearly, he couldn't hold his IPAs any longer without Carmella's influence. That should be paired with a march over to Finn's house and proper groveling on the front porch. They would invite him in for dinner, Shannon would regale him with stories of her class while Finn cooked, and then Rylie would coax him into building *another* sandcastle.

This was the way of things.

Rather, this was the way things *should* be.

But he didn't *wanna*.

Cue whining voice here.

Rob didn't want to go over to Finn and Shannon's house, didn't want to be coaxed into happiness by the joy in their little family. He didn't want to enjoy Rylie and all her exuberance, nor the way Shan and Finn so obviously loved each other.

He *wanted* to be miserable.

He'd perfected the art of being miserable, had it down to a science, especially once he added in a pinch of self-loathing and a dash of punishment, just for good measure.

But as he sat there and watched the sun set and the stars grow brighter, he had to wonder what was so good about it.

*Nothing.*

"I know," he whispered to Carmella, to that voice in his head. There *wasn't* anything good about it, nothing healthy or respectable or noble. He was miserable, and it was bleeding over into his family and friends' lives.

"You know what?"

The voice had his gaze jerking up, thankfully now lukewarm tea sloshing over the rim of the mug and coating the outside of his hand. Then he nearly dropped the mug altogether.

Because it was *her*.

The mystery woman.

# FOUR

# WRAPPING PAPER AND BATON TWIRLING

Soph

SHE PROBABLY SHOULDN'T BE HERE.

She certainly shouldn't be intruding on the poor man's quiet thoughts, making him slosh tea over his hand and down his pant leg.

She *definitely* shouldn't have stayed up into the wee hours of the night feeling bad for Rob.

But she had.

So she had tested the ten-minute theory of Finn's and had found him correct.

It had taken her all of seven minutes and thirty-six seconds to drive from her rental on the beach back over to Rob's house.

Just a drive-by, she'd assured herself, just out of blatant curiosity to test Finn's assertion, not because she wanted to catch a glimpse of Rob when he was sober. Certainly not so she could apologize for cursing him out on what had been a tough day—no matter that it had been done mechanically, fear driving every sharp word. Because she could have killed him, and then relief had mixed in and—

Kablooey.

She'd exploded.

And for a person in her position, that was dangerous. If it got out that she was verbally assaulting strangers she'd almost hit with her car . . .

Well, she didn't want to be branded that way.

Even if she *was* that way.

*Either* way, she owed the man an apology.

The last realization was what had propelled her from her car when she'd driven by and had seen him sitting on his front porch.

Now she could add almost squashing him, disturbing his quiet, *and* interrupting his private thoughts to her list of transgressions.

Though transgressions were the last thing on her mind when he stared at her.

His eyes, but lord, they were beautiful.

Tiger's eyes. They reminded her of those glimmering, swirling brown and amber and gold stones, their colors churning together in a pool to form the most unique combination of shades she'd ever seen.

They were striking, gleaming out at her.

But they also held a deep well of pain, and she remembered abruptly, almost jarringly, what had propelled her out of her car.

His wife.

His late wife.

And this grieving man.

She opened her mouth to apologize, to give her sympathies, but then those gemstone eyes hardened, and her words got stuck in her throat.

"I—"

"Don't apologize," he said, setting the mug down with a *plunk*.

"Wh-what?" she asked, stupidly she knew. But how had the man known she was going to apologize?

*Probably because you nearly ran him over with your car, dumbass.*

Well, there was that.

Her lips parted, that apology still on the tip of her tongue, but then she saw the knowing expression in those gorgeous eyes, the slight smirk on the edges of his mouth. The man thought he knew her.

That *he* knew *her*.

She wasn't easy to read—her childhood had disabused her of that notion, early and often. Hell, she'd gotten into acting because she was so damned good at hiding what was deep inside —whether it be painful parallels between her character and her upbringing or a co-star who'd decided it was a good idea to have fish for lunch before a kissing scene. Soph was a fucking profes- sional at obscuring her real emotions, and it was part of what made her so damned successful—she could easily project what the director asked for, what the script deemed necessary without letting ego or pesky feelings get in the way.

All fiction.

Every last tear and lovestruck sigh and passionate kiss.

Even with Finn—who was definitely *not* the co-star who'd had the fish.

*Shudder.*

"I can't take it," he whispered, his eyes sliding from hers, locking on something over her shoulder with such intensity that she nearly spun around to check. Then she realized he was less observing and more . . . deep in thought. "Everyone looks at me and only sees her," he whispered. "Which would be fine, if only I didn't miss her so fucking much." He dropped his head into his hands, lightly massaging his temples. "But fuck, I *do* miss her. So much."

The pain in him called to the pain in her, slicing her to the quick, making her remember all too much.

Frantically, she shoved down the memories, the hurt, the agony of knowing that life would never be the same because while the rest of the world went on, her world hadn't.

Just as this man's wouldn't.

His eyes flashed up to hers, and that pain inside her slipped its hold, escaped the box, and flooded out.

*God,* it hurt.

God, it made her *furious.*

Why had she come here? Why had she allowed this man to make her *feel?* He was a fucking stranger, who had absolutely no bearing on her life and—

Something inside her snapped.

Not control, since that had already slipped its hold, freeing those thoughts she'd purposefully locked away nearly twenty years before, but her . . . civility, she supposed, her sympathy, her pity.

That band holding tight to everything that was human inside her gave way.

She crossed her arms, leaned back against the porch post, and smirked down at him. "Why would I apologize to the dumbass who all but jumped in front of my car?" she sneered. "I should have run you over and saved the world the trouble of erasing you from its surface."

That fury gripping her was gone by the time she'd finished the words, like a wave sucked out to sea, and in the flow of the next one crashing ashore, colliding with her skin and cooling her to her core, it brought with it . . . shame.

And *fuck,* that burned, scalding her insides and somehow turning them to frost.

But then he smiled.

Or if not smiled, then at least one half of his mouth curved up, tilting in, revealing a tiny dimple in his cheek.

Would he have a pair if he smiled fully?

Would she ever have the chance to see it?

No.

No, of course, she wouldn't. She didn't deserve it, certainly, because insulting this man was like kicking a puppy and made her no better than—

*No.*

She'd thought that same word seconds before, hundreds if not thousands of times in the course of her life, but never with that amount of intensity, as though it had been torn from the very innards of her soul.

No, she could *never* be like them.

Never.

"I'm sorry," she whispered. "I shouldn't have—" Shaking her head as she spun around, she hurried down the three steps that led to the walkway, her heels clicking along the way, rushed along that straight shot of concrete, and turned—

Then was hauled to a stop, her hair flying forward to cover her face, a male chest very close to her spine, his spicy scent surrounding her.

"Wait," he said, his hot breath blowing against the back of her ear.

She shivered but didn't wait, just yanked her arm from his grip and started walking to her car.

He appeared in front of her a moment later, not touching her but definitely blocking her path. And stealing her breath because he was tall, rugged, and looking at her with his pretty eyes.

Her fucking kryptonite—a pair of eyes that held so many secrets.

"Wait," he said again.

She took a step, stopped.

But that only brought her in contact with him, with his chest, with his maleness, with . . . her guilt.

"I'm sorry," she whispered again. "I shouldn't have said that. Please forgive me."

An apology, not because she was worried about her brand or felt pity for this man. An apology because she felt like a caustic shrew who was taking out whatever nonsense was in her head on this man, who absolutely didn't deserve it.

Because he was nice and kind and sad, and the hurt little girl in her wanted to ruin that.

To cut it to shreds, to eviscerate that niceness, to make him pay just because he was a nice person.

And she was not.

Rob studied her for a long moment then his hand lifted.

Suddenly, abruptly, jerking up toward her face.

Sophie flinched.

Twenty years free of her nightmare didn't mean that her instincts were gone completely, no matter how carefully and deeply she had buried them. Twenty years didn't mean she'd forgotten what it felt like to have a palm cracking against her jaw, the sting that always followed, but on a one-second delay. Nothing but shock before that hurt bloomed on her cheek, burning along her nerves and spreading out like a flood.

His fingers had brushed her jaw, lightly, oh so lightly, before he appeared to register her reaction.

But she knew the moment he did, because those tiger's eyes darkened, and his hand slowly dropped to his side.

Slowly. Carefully.

Sympathetically.

Pityingly.

"Don't," she whispered, the word almost a hiss of sound. "Don't," she said again, echoing his earlier words. "I can't take it when—"

She bit down hard on her tongue, sucked in a breath.

Then lifted her chin, forced her tone to be neutral, if a little formal. "I apologize for nearly hitting you with my car." Soph sidestepped him, took one stride past his muscled form, past the man who'd seemed to become a statue, then she remembered what was in her purse and paused. Reaching inside, it took her fingers a moment to find the small package she'd wrapped carefully that morning. "Happy Birthday," she said, her tone deliberately cheerful, even as she didn't move from her position facing away from him, and he didn't move from his position facing away from her.

Two statues, or maybe like two runners, passing a baton. The air moved, his body shifted, and then his chest was once again at her back, taking up that baton-passing position in reality.

She didn't mirror him, didn't turn to see him.

She *couldn't.*

Instead, she fumbled for a moment, thrusting her arm back farther, jamming the present into his stomach, waiting for the weight to shift so she knew he'd grasped it, then releasing the small box and hurrying away.

Escaping.

Or maybe running. Either way, she'd gotten damned good at both over the years.

Only this time, instead of hustling away from her past, from the memories and the hurt and the discomfort, with nothing but the clothes on her back, a broken arm, a broken body, and bruises along every inch of her, she was *click-clicking* away in heels, with a designer handbag, and professionally whitened teeth, cut and colored hair, makeup to perfectly complement her coloring.

And still riddled with bruises.

Only they didn't show.

Because they were on the inside.

# FIVE
## EROSION = GOOD

Rob

HE STARED at the package in his hand, gaily wrapped with bright-patterned birthday paper, then glanced up and watched the mystery woman walk away.

Something jabbed at him inside his brain, prompting his lips to part, his throat to work, and his tongue to blurt out, "What's your name?" And he thanked God when she stopped and turned around, when she glanced back and looked at him for a long moment, that his mouth had run away with him.

Otherwise he wouldn't have realized he didn't know her name.

Wouldn't know the name of this tempest—wind flying and lightning sparking in all directions, and at the center . . . an emptiness that called to him.

Because it was the same emptiness that was inside him.

And in a heartbeat, he knew he was forever changed, that like a storm bearing down on an island might wash away a beach, the land abutting the ocean irrevocably changed. This woman had done that to the very fabric of his being.

Ridiculously poetic, he knew.

But also . . . true.

This woman was the first to smack him into reality.

All because he'd had a glimpse of that hurt inside her, because it mirrored his, because it made him feel . . . because she'd all but smacked him alongside the head and made him remember that he wasn't the only one who was in pain.

Pathetic it had taken him so long.

But then again, Carmella had always said he was as hard-headed as she was stubborn.

Two peas in a pod.

Surprisingly, the memory of his late wife didn't hurt. It was warmth and comfort and . . . a relief to be able to think of her in that way.

Not stubborn.

But happy and teasing.

"Soph," the woman in front of him said, and he focused on her face, judging her expression, seeing that she had hidden her pain carefully away. "Sophie Jackson."

Their gazes held.

Then with a small nod, she turned, got into her car, and drove away.

Leaving him on the sidewalk, holding a birthday present.

The first one he'd received since Carmella died.

And also the first time since Carmella had died that he didn't feel sliced clean down to the bone from the pain of his memories.

Tearing his eyes from the now empty road, Rob turned for the house, grabbed his mug of tea—now also cold—and headed inside, not bothering to lock the door behind him (because Stoneybrook) as he went into the kitchen.

He set the present on the counter, ignoring it for the time being, as he moved to the stove and turned on the kettle.

Then ignored it some more as he washed his mug out, grabbed a fresh tea bag from the canister in the cupboard, and made himself another cup. He'd long since given up caring that it wasn't a "manly" drink, and he certainly had enough hair on his chest to not need to drink coffee for that purpose. *Ha.* But truthfully, he couldn't care less for the taste of the black brew and would take his tea any day of the week.

Still ignoring the package as the tea bag soaked in hot water, he added a splash of milk then waited for it to cool down enough for him to drink.

But eventually—halfway through that mug—he knew his curiosity was going to get the better of him. Or perhaps *had* gotten the better of him was more accurate. He moved back to the kitchen island, picked up the palm-sized present.

It was light and small, and he wondered what the mystery woman, what *Soph* might have gotten for a man she didn't know, their only interaction, short, drunk, and filled with vomit.

Embarrassment hit like a Mack truck, reminding him that she'd done all the apologizing, that he hadn't made amends for stepping out in front of her car.

For not moving.

More embarrassment.

More shame.

He'd thought it would be so easy, just to let things go, to slip into that peaceful oblivion of light and shadows and rest.

Now, he knew differently.

He would never be at peace unless he was able to say goodbye to his wife.

Which meant he had some outstanding apologies stacking up.

Slipping his finger under the edge of the paper, he tugged up on the corner, feeling tape give way, the wrapping tear.

"Fuck," he whispered.

Inside that gaily covered present, the box was topped with a Post-It.

*I wasn't sure what was your favorite. But this one's mine.*

*-S*

He peeled back the slip of paper, revealing a small box of tea. The brand, the flavor that also happened to be *his* favorite.

Knees shaking, he sank onto a barstool, heart pounding, palms sweating.

Tempest. Sweeping in. Changing the landscape.

Changing *him*.

*She's a good one, my love.*

And somehow, Rob knew that would be the last time he heard his wife's voice inside his mind.

Because that tempest had shown him the way.

Things needed to change.

*He* needed to change.

---

IT WAS hard to pack up Carmella's belongings.

Painful to throw away her hairbrush, her makeup and brushes. Agony to clean out her nightstand and find all the little trinkets she'd kept.

Notes from him, from her parents. Birthday and Christmas cards.

A diamond necklace from her mom. A watch from her dad that had once belonged to her grandmother. Pictures of her from when she'd been a child.

Those were a little easier to stow, because he knew he could set them aside and put them in the box he would deliver to her parents. The things *he'd* bought for her were more difficult.

But the worst?

The clothes.

Because so many of his memories were tied up with the things she'd worn. Her prom dress, the sweater she'd worn when they'd finally gotten the keys to this place and had moved in, her wedding dress, the slinky black number she'd worn to celebrate them beginning to try to have kids.

Each hanger seemed to bring a new remembrance, a new pin into his heart, a new ache in his soul.

By the time he'd carefully packed her clothes away to donate, minus a few items he thought her parents would want, he felt wrung out but ready to tackle the next.

Her jewelry.

Or in reality, her engagement ring and wedding band.

Probably, he should donate it, should pass it on to someone who might need it, or sell it and donate the money. But in the end, he decided to tuck it safely in with the single nice watch he owned.

That was the piece of Carmella he'd keep.

He glanced down at his hand, at the gold band on his ring finger, and heart heavy but finally healing after all this time, he tugged the metal circle free and placed it in between those glittering rings.

Then he closed the drawer.

The way was forward, not back.

# SIX
## A SCARF AND A SWEATER

Soph

SHE HADN'T NEARLY RUN anyone over with her car in the last two weeks, so things were looking up.

Or maybe that was just the power of this town, the ocean, the soft sand beneath her toes.

Because she definitely saw the appeal that Finn had been droning on about while filming their movie and during the subsequent press tour. She'd chalked it up to him missing his wife, hadn't quite believed in the magic of this quaint East Coast town. But she'd been wrong.

It was absolutely magical.

Take now, the streets she was walking down. They looked like something she'd find on a set. Small buildings clustered together, white Craftsman-style pillars in front of each store, cute wooden awnings, their fronts holding a sign for each restaurant or storefront.

*Bert's Burgers*
*Mocha's Coffee and Bakery*
*Tangled: Yarn Emporium*

*Socks and Stuffies*

They all had cute names and adorable or tasty things inside she wanted to buy or eat. Or both. Hell, she wanted it all. But maybe first—she hesitated in front of the yarn store, her eyes drawn to a gorgeous sweater in the window, to the shades of purple changing from lavender to a deep purple in a striking ombre—she would take up knitting.

She had time on her hands. She could make a sweater, right? Although, realistically, she supposed she should start with a scarf.

But . . . maybe the sweater was on sale?

Smiling and enjoying her mental back and forth, she pushed into the shop, the tinkling bell signaling her presence to the shopkeeper—and boy was *that* an old-fashioned name for the bright and vibrant woman sorting through yarn at the counter.

"Hi, there," she said to Sophie. "How can I help you?"

"Hi," Soph said, almost as brightly. "I was just admiring that sweater in the window and was wondering if you have any . . . patterns or kits, I guess, for beginners? I'm wanting to learn how to knit."

"Ooh," the woman said, stepping out from behind the counter, her long blond ponytail giving weight to the shop's name.

Tangled.

Rapunzel.

Long, shining blond hair to match.

"I'm Sophie," she said, sticking out her hand, introducing herself, mostly in order to gain the woman's name and to prevent an accidental blurting of "You remind me of Rapunzel." Though, based on the tongue-in-cheek name of the store, it clearly wouldn't be the first time that had happened.

"Misty," she said with a smile, shaking Soph's outstretched hand. "You visiting?"

Soph nodded. "Just in town seeing friends for a few weeks."

"How lovely." Misty released her hand. "Let me show you around and get you set up."

"Thank you so much." Sophie followed her to the far wall where the yarn was arranged in clear acrylic bins, grouped by color, and forming the most beautiful rainbow she had ever seen in her life. She didn't know how to knit but was fighting the urge to go grabby hands on every roll of yarn she could reach as she listened to Misty tell her about the beginner patterns the store carried and the basic supplies she would need.

Maybe she could buy another suitcase to bring home her spoils of yarn?

There had to be a travel store in this town, what with all the cute shops selling their adorable wares, and she couldn't be the first person wondering how she was going to bring home everything she was about to buy.

"I think I like that one," Sophie said when Misty held out a selection of scarf patterns.

"Oh, that's lucky," Misty said, placing the chosen pattern in the basket she'd grabbed. "If you're going to be in town for a couple of weeks, I'm teaching—"

The bell rang, and they both turned to see . . .

Soph's heart squeezed hard, and the air froze in her lungs as Rob entered the store.

He pushed through the door, closing it quietly behind him, his gaze going directly to Sophie's and holding.

"Hey, Rob," Misty said. "I'll be right with you." She smiled at Soph. "So, as I was saying, I'm teaching a class to make this pattern, starting tomorrow and Thursday and then again next Tuesday and Thursday, if you're around that long."

"I would love to take a class," Sophie admitted. "I'm likely to muck up without help."

"Well, I can certainly help," Misty told her with a chuckle.

"Why don't you pick out three skeins of yarn, whatever color you'd like, and I'll check back in with you about needles."

"Thank you," she said then remembered the sweater. "Oh, I'm sorry, I meant to ask earlier. Is the sweater in the window for sale?"

Misty shook her head. "I'm afraid not, but I do sell the pattern."

"Great, thanks," she said, forcing a smile despite the disappointment filling her. Ridiculous, since it was just a sweater and she was certain she could get Misty to help her buy the yarn to make it.

Frankly, it was good practice for her not to get everything she wanted, not to be coddled. For a salesperson to not be all like, let me get that for you, Ms. Jackson Hollywood self. Hell, she couldn't remember the last time she'd been told no.

Plus, now she had a project to move toward.

Hashtag, life goals, etcetera, etcetera.

In the meantime, she deliberately turned her back on Rob and Misty, ignoring the bolt of jealousy that slid through her when she hugged him tightly and they began talking softly.

She didn't know the man, didn't have any reason to feel jealous.

Nope. No, sir. No way—

Oh look, *that* was a pretty purple, maybe even the same color as the sweater. Perhaps she could make her own ombre, just in scarf form, for practice.

Colors selected, she headed to the counter, both drawn to and dreading the man still standing there chatting with Misty. The pretty blonde halted the conversation, took Soph's basket, and gave her a brief run-down on needles so she could select a set. When Soph slipped away, Misty and Rob began talking in earnest, making her ears prickle, wanting to know what he was saying, even though she shouldn't care.

Having returned to the counter with two pairs—a deep mahogany wooden set and a pretty acrylic couplet, since she couldn't decide between them—Misty began ringing her up, and she got a glimpse into the serious discussion.

A bathroom remodel.

Which made her feel better. They weren't planning a date or a secret affair. They were talking about pipes and cold water and a sink faucet.

"How do I sign up for the class?" she asked when Misty and Rob paused in their conversation about a late shipment of tile.

"I'm sorry," Misty said, "that was terribly rude of me to jabber while you're waiting." Her lips quirked. "You clearly heard I'm redoing my bathroom, and it's been . . ." She bit her lip. "Well, it hasn't gotten off to the best start."

"It's been a disaster," Rob said, not mincing words. "We found mold and dry rot and had to tear out the entire floor, then the plumber installed not one, but two dysfunctional valves, and now her tile is delayed three weeks."

"Oh no," Soph said. "Do you at least have another bathroom you can use?"

Misty winced. "I've been showering here at the shop." A shrug, her eyes flicking to Rob's then away, cheer immediately returning to her face. "At least, I have a toilet again."

Now Rob winced. "I'm sorry, Dew Drop."

Soph's heart clenched at the nickname, at the obvious affection between the pair, even as she told herself she was an idiot to even feel that way.

"Hush," Misty said. "It's not your fault."

Rob grinned. "I think it's your right as a paying customer to complain when your contractor doesn't finish a job on schedule."

"Meh." A shrug. "You're doing the best you can."

"Still, feel free to yell at me like any other customer."

"I love you." She pressed a kiss to Rob's cheek. "But there will be no yelling. Plus," she said, lightly punching his shoulder, "I can always bum a shower at my big bro's house."

Relief.

It slid over Sophie like a cool compress pressed to a feverish forehead, slowly soaking in, filling her with respite.

Because the relationship hadn't been obvious until that moment, but then Soph couldn't believe how she'd missed it. The lines of their faces, their eyes—so unique with that swirl of amber and chocolate and gold mixing together.

"It's good to have options," Soph said with a smile, feeling more relieved than she should that the pair were related. "Especially when it means he can't reasonably say no."

It was convenient; that familial relationship made it easier for her to not have to examine the depth of her jealousy all that closely.

"True," Misty said, then bent and retrieved a binder from beneath the counter. "So, you'll be around for the class?"

"Yup." Sophie nodded. "Thanks for mentioning it." Then she paused, lips twitching when she saw the color of the binder, unable to stop herself from saying, "You like purple, don't you?"

"How could you tell?" Misty deadpanned, holding up the gorgeous purple binder, along with a purple pen. Her voice dropped to a whisper, her mouth turned up into a smile. "I may be a tad obsessed."

"You made the sweater for yourself." Sophie tilted her head toward the window.

Pink on Misty's cheeks. "I did," she said. "That's why I can't bear to sell it. I'm sorry."

Soph reached over and squeezed her hand. "*Don't* apologize. You're allowed to have nice things and to keep them." A smile. "I'm sure it took you ages to make, so you should at least be able to enjoy it!"

Misty blushed harder, flipping through the pages of the binder. "Ah—I— um . . . thank you for saying that."

"You're welcome," Soph said and let her gaze wander away from Misty as she began filling out a form, just so happening to catch Rob's, to get snared in his swirling brown eyes.

"Thank you," he mouthed, and she felt warmth slide through her.

"Okay." Misty set the paper in front of Sophie, along with the purple pen. "If you'll just fill out the rest of this, I'll bag up your items, and—"

The bell rang.

"Go," Rob told her as a trio of older ladies walked through the door. "I'll finish helping Sophie."

"Thanks, big bro," she said with a kiss to his cheek. "I'll owe you."

"We'll call it even." A beat. "Especially after the tile."

"And the toilet," Soph said, unable to stop herself from interjecting, even though it wasn't her place.

But luckily the siblings were amused—Rob snorting, his eyes dancing with amusement, Misty giggling as she walked over to help her new customers.

"Your sister is sweet," she murmured into the quiet that descended.

Rob finished scanning the yarn and pattern, placing them carefully into a paper bag that looked to be hand-stamped with a rendering of Rapunzel's tower made out of yarn.

Tangled.

So stinkin' cute.

"She certainly is," he said. "That will be sixty-eight sixty-two."

She passed over her credit card, signed the slip, and waited as he put her receipt into the bag and handed it over.

"Oh, wait." He took the bag back, pulled out a packet of

papers, and stuck them in along with her supplies. "For the class," he told her when she glanced at him in confusion. "Misty put together an intro and supply list and"—he shook his head, lips curving—"apparently a textbook on the subject of knitting."

"That's lovely." She reached for the bag.

He held it out of reach.

She lifted a brow, extended her arm a bit farther to grab it.

He backed up a step.

She huffed, going from touched by their relationship of this man helping out his sister with nary a thought, to annoyed. At this man. Because despite her best efforts, she liked him. And he was tormenting her, keeping her in his presence longer when she couldn't afford to want a relationship with him. Clenching her teeth together, she barely managed to stop herself from stomping her foot. "Did you need something?"

"No." A slight smirk on that gorgeous mouth.

Any whiff of attraction disappeared. The man was infuriating, staring down at her like he was in on a joke and she was the butt of it.

"Give me the bag," she gritted.

"No."

Now she *did* stomp her foot, luckily not too loudly since her heels were low and light, but the motion and the noise were loud or obvious enough for his eyes to flick down . . . then slowly trace back up.

Heat.

Okay, so maybe that attraction hadn't disappeared.

"You always wear heels?"

She was short and curvy. The heels elongated where she needed lengthening and added height so people didn't tower over her. They made her feel strong and powerful.

So, yes, she always wore the heels.

Except when a role called for something different or she was hiking or on the beach.

But walking around town, shopping until her heart was content?

Yes, her feet were happy in their heels.

"What's it to you?" she muttered.

He shrugged, leaned against the counter, her bag held captive in his arms. "I'm just curious, is all."

"Yes, I wear heels. Most of the time, anyway," she settled on saying.

His lips quirked. "I see."

Confusion drew her brows together. "*What* do you see?"

"Thank you for the birthday present."

"I—um—" She scrambled to adjust to the change in conversational topic. "Uh—you're welcome."

He shifted, his hip going to the corner of the counter, one hand still holding her bag, while the other slipped into his back pocket, lifting his shirt slightly, exposing a sliver of delicious-looking skin. And suddenly she wanted him.

Badly.

Holy hell.

This wasn't good.

"Soph," he murmured.

Her eyes drifted up slowly, tracing the lines of his flat stomach, the way his T-shirt went a little tight at his pecs, highlighting his natural strength rather than the super tight, look-at-me-I'm-so-strong-type the gym rats in L.A. often wore. There was something incredibly intoxicating about the natural muscle, made from the labor of one's work, rather than the carefully crafted ones she had so often seen.

"Yeah?" she asked, when she finally managed to make it past the way the cotton clung to his biceps, stretched taut over his shoulders.

"It was my favorite."

Befuddled, her brows drew together. "What?"

"The tea," he said. "It's my favorite."

"No." She shook her head. "I wrote the note . . . I . . . um . . . it's *my* favorite."

Fingers brushing back a lock of her hair. "I said what I meant."

Her frown deepened. "I don't know *what* you meant."

"I meant, it's *my* favorite, too."

She blinked. It was? That was . . . odd.

"Oh," she murmured.

"Yes," he said. "*Oh.*"

Silence for a heartbeat, then he handed her the bag, thrusting it at her without warning so she scrambled to take hold of it, and their hands brushed, tangled—

Sparks alighting her skin.

Heat sliding between her thighs.

Desire pooling in her stomach.

She wanted this man.

*Wanted* him like she had perhaps never wanted another. No, not *perhaps.* She'd never felt this . . . *need* for another person. It was deeper than just sex—something she'd had plenty of over the years. Something she'd had *too* much of probably before she'd been able to untangle the way her past had played into that promiscuity, before she'd begun to respect herself enough for it to only be for her, instead of a desperation to erase the demons of her memories.

This was a different sort of longing. It was intense desire, but more. It was wanting to be near this man, to fall deep into his eyes and never come out.

And she hardly knew him.

Alarm bells blared.

"I . . . um . . . I should go." She nodded to the door.

He smiled gently. "Bye, Sophie."

Clutching the bag to her chest, she turned for the exit, wanting to run, wanting to stay, wanting to—

"I'll see you at class," he called.

She froze, glanced back.

He winked and smiled, slow and hot. "Turns out, I need to learn how to make a scarf, too."

"I—" She broke off. God, why were words so hard with this man? She was an actress, usually had no shortage of words. But he just . . . made them all poof away.

He just . . . made her want—

Something she couldn't.

So she didn't bother with the words, with continuing her attempts in summoning some up.

Instead, she fled, the bell tinkling behind her.

# SEVEN
## SISTERS. LE SIGH

Rob

"WHAT WAS THAT ABOUT?" Misty asked after she had taken care of the trio of permed ladies and come back to him at the counter.

"What do you mean?" he prevaricated, even while knowing *exactly* what she was talking about.

He didn't willingly engage in conversation with women—or at least, not with attractive women who might be construed as someone he might be interested in. Well, that wasn't entirely true. He'd tried a few dates, but none had gone well. He hadn't truly dated anyone besides Carmella. They'd gotten together in middle school, had been best friends before that. So, Rob had never needed to be charming or to flirt with another woman, never kissed, let alone slept with anyone besides her. So while the dates with the others (read: two women) hadn't exactly been a disaster (although close), he'd decided he wasn't in any position or mental shape to pursue that.

Or to put the poor woman who agreed to a date with a mess like him through that.

Rob had decided to wait until he had his shit more together.

Except, it had been two years, and he'd only just recently packed up his wife's hairbrush.

"I mean you—*Hey!* What are you doing?" Misty asked, probably finally noticing that he was making an addition to her purple binder. One he'd bought for her, along with the custom dividers and templates for signup forms, partly because he knew his planner obsessed sister would enjoy it, but also because he'd thought it might give her the push to finally pursue this dream of hers—to own her own shop.

It was a gift that he had been beyond pleased to see her using when she'd found the courage and *had* opened her store, just six months before Carmella's death.

Courage that shamed him now.

Because he'd been living under a cloud of fear for too long—keeping everyone at a careful distance, hanging on to the past, even while determinedly wearing a mask of *I'm perfectly fine.*

What better way to stave off those who'd pull him into the land of the living than to cheerfully push his family and friends away?

Except Finn *had* seen through him. Along with Shannon.

They hadn't invited him to eat or come over and watch a game or to BBQ on the beach so much as had *insisted* he come along, and with Rylie in their ranks, they'd had a clever ally. He hadn't been able to say no, and he supposed that some part of him—a corner peeling back on the strip of duct tape holding the pieces of his heart together—had wanted to get close to people again.

Thus, games and meals and the occasional beach BBQs.

Thus, the overindulgence at Carmella's grave.

Thus, the abject misery over the reality that his wife was never coming back.

Thus . . . Sophie.

Who had made the tape rip clean away, causing the pieces to fall apart, to thud resoundingly in his chest, the fragments reverberating with a weight they shouldn't have been able to carry. Only this time, Rob had found a determination to stitch himself together, to shed that weight.

Because of cursing and a box of tea.

Because of a voice in his head whispering encouragement.

"Rob," Misty exclaimed, trying to snatch the binder. "I asked, what the hell do you think you're doing?"

"I'm signing up for a class," he told her, brushing her hands away and filling out the form for a class titled—he shuddered —*Princess Knitting 1*. He signed his name at the waiver on the bottom with a flourish, then pulled out his credit card and rang himself up.

"I suppose I'll have to rename the class now," she grumbled.

He winked. "I'm fine with being a princess," he said. "So long as you can teach me how to knit a crown, too."

"I can." Her chin lifted. "But maybe instead of teaching you, I'll knit one for you and make you wear it during class."

He laughed.

She laughed then she hugged him, her tone going sober, her arms squeezing tight. "I'm glad you're back. I've missed you."

He frowned. "I've been right here."

Her eyes, a mirror of his own, drifted up to meet his, sadness tingeing the edges. "No, Robbie, no, you haven't." Then before he could allow the guilt swelling through him to bubble over into an apology, she spun around, picked up a basket, and headed to the wall of yarn.

"What are you doing?"

She glanced back, mouth quirking. "If you're taking the class, you're going to need supplies."

Since that was true, he waved a hand, "Carry on then."

A finger tapped against her chin. "I think you'd look lovely in a bright pink scarf."

"A true man is comfortable in every color." He sneakily flipped back a page in the binder as she turned to study the wall of yarn. "Pink away."

She snorted, pulled out a roll of something that looked to be smattered with silver sparkles and a plethora of bright pink colors, considered it for a moment, then put it in the basket.

Fine by him.

Misty pondering his torture meant that he could get the information he wanted.

By the time she'd finished, the slip of paper with Sophie's phone number was in his pocket, and he had stowed the binder away. Misty plunked the basket full of pink knitting needles and yarn and something that looked like plastic safety pins—also pink—on the counter, laying them out so he could see they matched perfectly with the pink bag she'd included, along with tiny pink scissors he questioned could actually fit on his fingers, a pink measuring tape, and what he thought he'd her call tapestry needles. They were about the length of his pinky finger —so scarily large—but shining steel instead of pink.

The one nod to his masculinity.

Or a threat to it, he thought with a smile, imagining his sister wielding those needles with precise concentration.

"Just necessary supplies," she said.

"I don't remember Sophie having this much," he pointed out as she began ringing him up.

A shrug. "Sophie wasn't in my binder, sneaking information about other clients."

Heat smothered his cheeks. "Not sure what you're talking about, Dew Drop."

"Hmm," she said, rapidly scanning the bunch, then in a quick move that he hadn't expected and thus, couldn't dodge, she reached into his pocket, snagged his wallet . . . and the piece of paper he'd stashed there. "Still not sure you know what I'm talking about?" she asked, holding it up.

He snatched both back, dug out his credit card, and handed it to her. "Yup," he muttered, shoving Sophie's number back into his wallet.

"Do you even know who that is?"

"She's . . ." He shrugged. "Sophie."

"No, big bro, *she's* Sophie Jackson." A beat, her eyes lifting when the name clearly didn't ring a bell. "The actress."

He shrugged, brow lifted. That wasn't a surprise, considering she knew Finn.

Misty sighed. "Sophie *Jackson*. The big-time actress with the number one film. The one who starred opposite of Finn and got *all* the awards."

He kept his brows lifted.

He hadn't seen the film, and he and Finn didn't discuss Finn's work. There were always other things to talk about— Shannon's students, the gossip in town, Rylie's copious knowledge of all things *Pokémon*.

"Ugh," Misty sighed. "You're hopeless."

"I think we established that already."

With another sigh, she ran his card for a truly exorbitant amount even based on the volume of pink she was shoving into a paper bag—but he signed the slip without complaint, took the sack when she thrust it at him. Then he just nodded when she scowled and snapped out, "Tomorrow. Six P.M. sharp."

"Thanks, sis." He leaned over the counter to press a kiss to her forehead. "I owe you one."

She narrowed her eyes. "Yes, you do."

"Well, if I'm in the hole already," he began. "I wanted to ask—"

"Nope." Her lips made a *popping* sound on the p. "The answer is no. N. O. No."

"Dew Drop," he began. "It's—"

For as sweet and softhearted as she presented herself to the outside world, Misty sure could give him an evil eye.

"It's not happening."

But he knew how to make her cave. Actually, it was easy really. All he needed to do was give her the look. The *sad, puppy dog* look that had once managed to get her to sacrifice her favorite Barbie to the clutches of his evil army men as a child and the expression he knew would get her to agree now. Because he knew the power of the *sad puppy dog* look and thus, he only used it judiciously.

He also knew it was going to work because the favor wasn't for him.

"Don't try to guilt me into this, mister," she began, crossing her arms over her chest, tossing her blond ponytail over her shoulder.

He made the *sad puppy dog* expression sadder . . . and puppier.

She groaned, spun away.

And victory was in the bag.

Resisting the urge to fist-pump, Rob knew that he owed it to his sister to lay his cards on the table. "Look, I've had a hard time of it," he said simply. "I know you've seen that. I know *everyone* has seen that. But I'm not blind, either. I know I've made it hard for you, too, and I'm sorry for that." A sigh, his voice gentling. "I just . . . I had a vision of this *life* with Carmella, and it's like I only got a glimpse of how wonderful it was going to be and . . ." He blinked, throat suddenly tight.

Misty rotated back to face him, her eyes the ones that were sad now—and not with his brand of fake hang-dog mien, but with real sadness. She covered his hand with hers. "Then suddenly it was gone," she said softly.

"Yes."

"I'm sorry," she whispered. "I know you and Carmella loved each other very much." She squeezed his hand lightly. "*I* miss her quite desperately. She was part of my life for so long that it feels like a void was left behind when she died, one that won't ever be filled." A sniff. "What I'm trying to say is that I understand how your grief would be so much more intense than my own."

He nodded, swallowed hard, and forced out, "Yeah."

She forced a smile. "So, you have absolutely nothing to apologize for. You're a good man, who hit a really rough patch. That's bound to cause some whiplash."

"I felt like I was in a fucking fog for these last years, like quicksand was sucking me down and I couldn't escape."

"It's okay, Rob."

"It's not okay," he said. "Yes, I lost Carmella, but the truth is that I should have been there for you instead of being stuck in this pattern of grief." He thrust a hand through his hair. "No, that's not true. I wasn't stuck. I didn't *want* to escape. I just wanted to be miserable. To not truly live if Carmella wasn't here."

Her throat worked, a tear sliding down her cheek. "Oh, Rob."

He wiped it away. "But . . ." God, how to even begin to explain this? How could he explain that he felt like the clouds had cleared after a long storm, the darkness slipping away, the sun shining brighter. He'd finally found the urge to live his life.

Not to forget. *Never* to forget.

Rather, to hold her close, but to also . . . maybe to have that potential of more again.

Probably, he should be terrified of caring about someone again.

Instead, he just wanted to *feel* again.

And he *had* started to feel again.

"Sophie bought me tea," he whispered.

"What?" Her eyes went wide. "How did she know—?"

"I don't know," he said. "But she showed up yesterday and gave me a birthday present."

Her mouth dropped open. "But we don't celebrate your birthday, not since—" She broke off.

He heard the words anyway. They didn't celebrate his birthday any longer. Not since Carmella had died on her way home from work, his favorite ice cream cake on the floor of the passenger seat, a wrapped gift in the back seat.

Rob had discovered the melted mass when he'd had to sign off on the car being totaled, along with the present, which was still wrapped, still sitting on a shelf in his closet.

"I know, Dew Drop," he said, blinking that away. "But I accepted the gift anyway. I should pretend I was just being polite, but the truth is I felt something when I saw her then. No, the truth is that I *feel* something when I'm with her, when I'm talking with her and . . . I wanted it and . . ."

Misty waited while he organized his thoughts.

"And when I opened it, inside was tea. *My* tea."

Her lips parted, a breath sliding out. "What do you mean *your* tea?"

"I mean the pomegranate blend Shelby makes in town." A beat. "Along with a note saying she hoped I enjoyed it, since it was her favorite."

She leaned back against the counter, eyes cautious. "That's . . . a strange coincidence."

"I know," he agreed. "But that combined with my drunk ass nearly getting run over by her car and then puking and passing out in front of her, and her knowing Finn and calling him for help to get me home, and I realized that I was stuck in this—"

"Wait, *what?*" Misty asked. "She almost ran you over and—"

Shit. That hadn't been a detail he'd planned on sharing. But his thoughts were swirling, his mind filled with . . . so much color and so many thoughts, and his mouth had run away with him—

Because the most important part was the piece he hadn't yet mentioned.

"I packed up Carmella's things."

Misty's inhale was sharp.

"It sounds fucking stupid, but it's like the moment I tore off that wrapping paper and saw what was inside, I realized everything I had been missing out on."

"Rob," she whispered.

"I'm sure this newfound lightness will shrink away at some point, that I'll regress back into being a moody asshole," he said.

"I hope not." Her hand covered his again. "I want you to be happy."

"I want that, too. Finally," he added. "I think I finally want that, too." He shrugged. "I think it's because Soph saw something in me." He laughed. "She was with me for hardly any time at all, and yet she managed to see beneath the surface, and I—I guess I just want to continue holding on to that feeling of someone seeing me as something more than this man who was broken." A beat. "Even if nothing more comes of it."

She sniffed again, another tear escaping.

He wiped it away. "I'm sorry. I didn't mean to make you cry."

A light punch to his arm. "Sure, you did," she said, or rather deliberately grumbled, making the wound inside his heart heal more, that light feeling that had begun with Sophie continue to expand. "You knew I'd become a watering pot the moment you brought out the *sad puppy dog* look."

"I'll neither confirm nor deny." He grinned. "I love you, Dew Drop."

"I'd love you more if you stopped using that nickname."

He tugged a strand of her hair. "Never gonna happen."

"Ugh. Such is the burden of younger sisters everywhere." Her chin came up. "Okay, bro. Lay it on me, what's this big favor you need of me?"

"Well," he said, "if you're really sure you're up for it."

Her eyes narrowed. "Rob," she warned.

"I was just wondering . . ."

# EIGHT
## DEFUNCT TOTE BAG STRAPS

Soph

SHE'D SPENT her day at the beach, her toes in the sand—and not in the water that was too chilly for her taste this time of year.

But the breeze had been fresh, the sun peeking out behind the clouds at regular intervals, and she'd enjoyed being able to step off her front porch, to plunk her ass into the sand, and then to lose herself in her favorite book.

Which, for her entire life, had always been the novel she was currently reading, and today was no different.

She'd devoured the historical romance then had lain back in the sand and sighed.

Over the happy ending—that only ever happened in books and on the silver screen.

But still, she loved the escapism and had especially loved the way the couple had found their way back to each other in the end. So much so, that she'd replayed the scene over and over in her head, mentally blocking out what it would look like if it were filmed, who she would cast as the hero to play opposite her.

Because, *of course,* she'd be the heroine.

Grand gestures were the most fun when they happened to her.

Even if they were just fiction.

Smiling, she rubbed a finger down her slightly sunburned nose, knowing that she'd spent too long lazily sprawled on the sand—lazily because she hadn't bothered with a beach towel or blanket or umbrella and certainly hadn't rustled up the energy to go back into her rented cottage for sunscreen. Nope. She'd been content with all of that laziness, and still was, even knowing that she hadn't gotten all of the sand out of her hair, despite the long shower she'd taken before class.

Class!

She was strangely excited for this small-town knitting class.

It wasn't like she hadn't taken her fair share of courses throughout the years, even ones in little shops like Tangled, though most of them had been in preparation for some role or another.

This was just for her.

Although she supposed it would probably find its way on screen at some point or another.

One of her characters could jab a bad guy with a needle. Or maybe, she thought, pulling into the small parking lot behind the shop, she'd just play a girl who liked to knit.

That was a possibility.

Although one that was less appealing than a fierce ninja badass.

Snorting, she began to turn into an empty spot, only to have her throat seize and her heart pound when she had to slam on the brakes in a hurry.

She screeched to a stop, nearly hitting . . . Rob.

For a second time.

He was crouched next to a truck, shielded from view, the

driver's door shut, and his body curled up as he reached under his truck to grab—

A knitting needle.

Which he held up triumphantly, flashing her a smile through her windshield.

She cursed, waved back, then waited for him to move before slowly—and exceedingly more carefully—pulling into the spot.

Then she took her time gathering her supplies, which she'd stowed in her favorite tote bag—a canvas number emblazoned with *Book Nerds Unite*. Old and stained and with a strap she'd reattached more times than she could count, it was something Soph couldn't give up. It had been the first thing she'd bought with her own money, the first time she'd saved up, the first time she'd realized she could get something she wanted all on her own.

And the first time she'd known that she was going to survive.

All because of a stupid bag.

Yet, the strip of canvas meant more to her than any designer purse she'd purchased in the following years.

After double-checking to make sure her wallet was inside, she slung her tote over her shoulder and took a deep breath before tugging at the handle and popping open her door.

She didn't jump at Rob's voice.

Probably because some part of her had assumed he was going to wait for her.

Or maybe because part of her had *wanted* him to be waiting for her.

"Hey, Soph."

Heated velvet skating over her skin, alighting along her nerves, raising the hairs on her arms, gooseflesh on her nape. Her thighs clenched together, and she was acutely aware of him standing just a few feet away, positioned at the rear of her car.

"Hi," she murmured, feeling oddly shy.

For God's sake, she'd been the one to drive over to his house, to give him the present. Why should she now be feeling reserved?

Except . . . something had changed between them.

He saw her as though . . . *he* saw *her*.

Like a man who'd seen a woman he wanted.

No longer was he the sad-eyed widower. Instead, he was all man, big and strong and staring at her with scorching predator-like focus.

That intensity made her want to run, to hide, to bury everything deeper.

Because he was no longer safe.

She could see that as easily as she was able to bring life to her characters on screen.

But she was an actress for a reason, could pull the shroud of falseness around her, hold it tight like a shield. She could disarm and charm even the grossest, grabbiest producer, slipping out from scenarios with nary an ill-gotten touch *and* their egos intact. Because Sophie had plenty of experience doing the same thing.

Avoid being cornered.

Avoid being put into a situation that would bring her harm.

Avoid being a victim.

And when she couldn't avoid all of that, she used her skills at deception to neutralize the threat.

*Then* she ran.

"It's lovely to see you again," she said, closing the door of the rental and locking it. "I was so happy to stumble upon your sister's store yesterday, it's rather . . ." She paused for a moment because she wasn't the type of woman to use a word like lovely —at least in this context—let alone a second time in as many sentences. She blamed historical romances for making her language old-fashioned, though she wouldn't be giving them up in her lifetime. ". . . adorable," she finished.

His lips twitched. "Yes."

"Misty and the shop both are," she said, nibbling the inside of her mouth and pondering how to get by him when he was taking up so much space at the back of her car.

She *could* slip by him. But that would bring her body very close to his.

She could retreat, round the hood of her car. But that would look a little ridiculous and like she was avoiding him.

Of course, she *was* avoiding him.

But she just wanted to pretend she wasn't.

Her foot slid on the parking lot's surface, shifting to step back, her heel making a soft scuffing noise that drew his gaze. It flicked down to her suede navy pumps before it worked its way back up to her face.

Soph swallowed.

There was no way around it. She'd round the front of the car and go inside, accept that he would know she was disquieted and—

"We should get to class," he said, turning to the side and retreating several paces, giving her plenty of room for her to slide between the cars and him, to not really even come close. "My sister is sweet and adorable, as you said. However, she does *not* appreciate late students," he added with a smile that was hot enough to melt some of the ice that had frozen her in place.

She shook off her nerves, nodded, and walked forward. "You're right."

A grin as she passed him. "Don't keep telling me that. I'll get a big head."

Now, it was her turn for her gaze to drop, to slide slowly south, to where she wondered if he had a big head *there,* too.

Then just as quickly, she shook herself, readjusted the strap on her bag and hurried across the parking lot.

*Click-click.*

*Click-click.*

*Thump. Thump.*

She glanced over, saw that he'd come up next to her. Fine, she'd already felt him closing the distance between then, the tingling awareness at the base of her neck, the way the tips of her fingers went itchy, wanting to touch.

But . . . seeing was almost as great as the feelings he evoked.

*Almost.*

She shook her head at herself, knowing it was a mistake to feed what was quickly becoming a need for this man—to see, to yearn to touch, to—

*Enough.*

Because it was a need she couldn't act on for a multitude of reasons.

And still, she let her gaze drift over to take in the strong shoulders and arms, the flat stomach and narrow hips, the muscled legs, the—

Pink sparkling bag he clutched in his hand.

More fear disappearing. More longing shifting in to take its place. Maybe he wasn't dangerous. Maybe he wouldn't hurt her. Maybe he would see her as more than her past and her present.

And those maybes had her murmuring, "Doesn't exactly go with your outfit."

He grinned. "As I said, my sister may look sweet and inno-cent"—he held up the bag—"but she has a mean streak."

"I happen to think that pink goes quite nicely with your complexion."

"A compliment." He waggled his brows. "I'll take it. Though," he added as they stepped onto the sidewalk in front of the shop, "I hope I'll get the same compliment on my yarn. It's somehow even more pink—"

His words cut off.

Probably because she'd stopped, disappointment coursing through her at the sight of the mannequin in the window.

It was wearing a different sweater.

The purple was gone.

She'd been planning on asking Misty once more that evening if she could purchase it. Just once more. She wasn't going to force the girl. It was just . . .

Pretty and she'd wanted it and—

Silly, huh?

"What is it?" Rob asked, his voice close enough to her ear to make her jump, even though it wasn't particularly loud.

Proximity.

Attraction.

Danger.

He straightened, and out of the corner of her eye, she watched him glance from her to the direction of her stare before she felt his gaze return to her face. "I—"

She blinked, forced herself to smile. "Sorry," she murmured. "I was woolgathering."

"Been known to do that myself a time or two," he said cheerfully.

Almost *too* cheerfully, considering she was suddenly feeling very grumpy about the sweater, even as she knew she was being ridiculous and telling herself it was just a sweater.

It was just . . . she'd even brought a signed script, hoping to tempt Misty, since it had one of the actors from her shop's namesake.

Bribery.

Yup, she was down to bribery.

But—

*It's my precious.*

Or at least that was what her inner Gollum kept saying. She'd dreamed about the damned sweater last night, imagining what it would feel like on her skin, how warm it would make her.

Wow.

Telling her inner ring-hoarding—or perhaps sweater-hoarding was more apt—brain to chill, she smiled at Rob and reached for the door.

He beat her there, tugging it open, the bell chiming, and marking their entrance to the circle of five women sitting in wooden chairs, a round, scarred table in the middle of them, a scattering of yarn and needles in front of them.

But that chaos and color and ten eyes on her wasn't what stole her focus.

No, that was the man next to her. The man who held the door, so she had to walk past him, forcing her to move close to him. To smell him. To feel him and the warmth of his body.

To *want* him.

Shuddering, she forced her gait to stay even.

But even then, he noticed her reaction.

"Cold?" he murmured, still very close, still filling up her senses.

No, she wasn't cold. Not in the least. In fact, she was quite hot, sweltering even, heat sliding through her limbs and coiling in her center.

"Hmm. Maybe next time you should wear a sweater."

Sweater.

He was telling her to wear a sweater.

And reminding her of *the* sweater.

Her Gollum-urges prickled.

Ugh.

Annoyed at herself, unreasonably annoyed at *him*, she

glanced over her shoulder. "Maybe you should mind your fucking business," she said so sweetly it was completely full of saccharine.

The man just smiled and shrugged. "You're probably right."

Then he moved to the table and took a chair.

The last empty one.

Seriously?

She glared.

He smiled and shrugged again.

She barely resisted the foot stomping. Again.

"Come, sit down," Misty called. "We have plenty of room." With that, she stood and dragged another chair into the circle, forcing the other women to shift and scoot as they made space for the new addition.

Next to Rob.

Sophie's gaze caught Misty's, and she lifted a brow.

Misty just smiled innocently, and since she didn't know the other woman well enough to know if it was truly an innocent action or if she were hiding her mischievousness beneath the surface of all that supposed goodness, Soph stifled a sigh and took her spot.

Next to Rob.

Even more unreasonably annoyed, she barely managed to portray calmness as she unpacked her knitting supplies. Hell, she didn't even really know why she was furious.

Certainly not about the sweater.

Nor the chair.

It was just . . . this man was sandpaper rubbing against her skin, exfoliating her nerves, bringing them to painful attention, making her want things she couldn't want, and—

Taking a knitting class, presumably because he wanted to be near her.

Which was sweet and—

Dangerous.

Definitely dangerous.

"Okay," Misty said, "now that we're all settled in, let's get started." Then she had everyone unfold their copy of the pattern and taught them how to read it.

Concentrating fiercely despite her awareness of Rob, she found that it wasn't too difficult, especially with Misty's cheat sheet of symbols and techniques for how to count stitches.

But despite her best intentions, it wasn't long before Soph was in over her head. Misty had instructed them how to cast on —which was basically step one of the knitting project and the term to get the yarn on the needles—and now they were supposed to be practicing the technique as she moved around the room.

Except, Soph was a mess.

Or maybe her yarn was.

Or perhaps they both were.

"Dammit," she muttered, yanking the yarn off, knowing that she'd have to wait until Misty made another round and showed her the method for a third time.

"Psst."

Slanting her eyes to the left, to Rob, to the manly mass of muscle that was probably the sole reason she was having a hell of a time concentrating, she hissed, "What?"

"Want help?"

Setting her yarn and needles down. "How could you possibly help—"

Her words faltered because the blasted man had already cast on and had a good six rows of scarf hanging from his needles.

She clenched her jaw.

He shrugged, that casual lift and drop of his shoulders she decided she'd already seen enough of for a lifetime.

"I thought you wanted to *learn* how to knit a scarf."

So help her God, if he shrugged, she'd take this knitting needle and—

The man must have recognized the precariousness of his situation because he smiled. "Maybe I meant I needed to know how to knit *this* scarf." A beat as she continued to glare. "Do you want help or not?"

Wanted?

No.

Needed? Her stare flicked between his project and her own.

Obviously, yes. If she was ever going to get this scarf going, she needed someone's help, and since Misty was currently helping a brunette with round turquoise glasses and consternation on her face, while another woman with pale blond hair and eyes to match was next up for assistance, Soph knew her options were limited.

Receive help from this man, who unnerved her in the most uncomfortable—okay, also delicious and dangerous way—*or* to get his help.

But she didn't *wanna*.

For better or worse, he took her reluctance as acceptance.

"Here," he said, sliding his chair closer to hers and lightly grasping her hands in his. "You hold the needle like this—" His fingers shifted hers, the roughened pads making her shiver and he glanced down at her. "Cold?"

She shook her head, her gaze drawn to the lower corner of his mouth, to a tiny white scar that marked it like a tally mark, to the glimpse of a dimple on his cheek.

"Now," he murmured, that voice soft but moving like liquid heat over her skin, as though she were dipping one leg then another then sliding her entire body into a steaming bath. "You bring the yarn over like this"—a pause, his tiger's eyes meeting hers and holding—"with me so far?"

Forcing herself to concentrate, she focused on the movement of his hands, his fingers feeding the yarn up and over, bringing the needles through, guiding her own hands along with his.

"That's it," he said after a few minutes, releasing her. "Now, you've got it."

She kept going, knitting another stitch and then another, this time without his help.

Were they the neatest stitches she'd ever seen? No.

Were they as neat as the ones he'd guided her through? Also no.

But they were made by her own hands, and before long, she had the first piece of a scarf. That *she* was going to make.

Pride—probably way too much for the pittance of stitches that were actually on her needle—bloomed through her, filling her with something akin to helium, making her feel as though she could float up to the ceiling and stay there, casually coasting above the room, grinning down at everyone, and chanting, "I made this! I made this!"

Pushing the thought aside and biting back a smile at her ridiculousness tugging up the corners of her mouth, she returned to the task at hand—knitting this damned scarf.

And Rob sat next to her, pink needles working on the pink yarn, occasionally murmuring a direction when she paused to glare down at her work of . . . art? Not precisely, but even as lumpy and uneven as it was, at least it had pretty colors and would keep her neck warm—

*Hopefully*, she thought, tugging out a few stitches when she realized she was about to leave a gaping hole in the length.

"What made you want to be an actress?" he asked, drawing her attention from the tangled yarn.

She lifted a brow. "Small talk now?"

A shrug, his fingers moving smoothly enough that she

knew there was no way the man should be in a beginning knitting class. "I was recently informed that you're kind of a big deal."

"And what?" she asked, feeling a curl of bitterness. "Now, you're all of a sudden interested in me?"

His mouth quirked. "Nope."

Just nope.

And *pop* there went her ego, deflated like a balloon, her out-of-body experience, her ceiling floating and hissing away as she drifted back down to reality.

Nope.

N. O. P. E. *Nope.*

Cool.

"I fell into acting, decided I liked it enough to move to L.A.," she said to fill the silence, or maybe to cover up the sound of all that ego *pfting* away into space. "Then after quite a few years of being a working actress, I got that lucky break like so many people dream of."

"Wow."

She shrugged. "Sometimes, going to buy a cup of tea can change a person's life."

He froze for long enough that she went over what she'd said, trying to discern what had put such a stark expression on his face. Then his shoulders dipped. "One small moment, a chance encounter." A nod. "Yes, sometimes they can absolutely make the biggest changes in people's lives."

Her breath caught. "What was the change in yours?" she found herself asking.

Then immediately clamping her teeth together to contain her groan.

She was such a dumbass.

Soph opened her mouth, an apology on the tip of her tongue, but Rob spoke first, and he surprised her. "Overalls," he said softly, staring down at the beginnings of the pink scarf on his pink needles.

"What?" she asked.

His eyes flicked to hers. "Overalls changed my life." A small smile. "Or at least an idiotic boy grabbing onto the straps and hauling Carmella, hauling my late wife around." He grinned. "When she was in kindergarten, that was. But regardless, it allowed me to sweep in and save the day."

"What did you do to the idiotic boy?"

A shrug. "Stole his favorite ball and threw it onto the roof of the school."

She giggled. "Devious."

"Not really," he said. "Truthfully, I didn't even think. I was just so pissed that I yanked the ball from his grip and yeeted it right up onto that roof." He paused, straightened a portion of her yarn that had gotten tangled. "Probably for the best that I chose that instead of pushing or hitting him. Not only was he a giant baby—as most bullies are wont to be—but he was the biggest tattletale in school."

"I hate bullies," she said. "So, it sounds like he got what he deserved."

"That's what I tried to tell the other kids, when they realized I'd gotten rid of our class's only good four-square ball." His expression was filled with amusement. "But that was another one of those moments that change a life."

"How?"

"Carmella stood up for me." A beat. "And brought in a new room ball, courtesy of her allowance."

Sophie laughed. "How old were you guys?"

"Five? Maybe six?"

"And you stayed friends?"

"*Best* friends," he said. "And then boyfriend and girlfriend."

"And eventually husband and wife." She nodded. "How

amazingly lucky for you both to have found each other so early."

He opened his mouth, paused, then sighed. "I've never thought about it that way."

She fumbled with her needles and yarn, trying not to drop both, then managed to find his hand and squeeze it lightly. "Sorry if I—"

Flipping his palm over, he tangled his fingers with hers. "No, don't apologize. It's nice to be able to talk about her without hurting so much."

"I'm glad."

They sat there for a moment, hands laced together, eyes locked, and . . . Sophie forgot how to breathe, or maybe it was just her heart malfunctioning as it pounded beneath her rib cage.

*Thud-thud.*

*Thud-thud.*

*Thud-thud.*

His lips parted. "Do—"

"All right, everyone." Misty's voice broke in on whatever Rob had been about to say, and she would have given her lumpy scarf to hear the rest of his statement.

But then he pulled back slightly, and she returned her hands to her lap.

"That's it for class today," Misty went on. "Please, stay after if you have any further questions. Thursday, we'll go into detail about the middle section of the scarf, which is a different stitch." She chuckled. "So, your homework—or mission, should you choose to accept it—is to finish the top block. Thanks, everyone!"

A beat of quiet as goodbyes and gratitude were exchanged and the class cleared out, one or two of the other students hanging around afterward to talk with Misty.

Soph felt Rob's gaze on her as she packed away her things, a heated and almost tangible thing, but still unnerving. Mostly because she liked it so much. To like a man, to *truly* like him, or even more frightening, to *love* him was dangerous and too risky for her blood.

She didn't think she would ever marry, didn't think she was capable of tying herself to someone that way.

Not after what she'd escaped.

So no, no husband, no kids, nothing more than friends, and even those who got close to her had to survive an odious quest to penetrate her walls, only the most persistent and rigorous making their way to the prized possession of her friendship.

Ha.

Prized possession.

Now *that* was her Hollywood ego talking.

She was no gift, no gem, no glorious treasure at the end of a long, arduous journey. She could play nice on the surface, give a great interview, but Soph was too closed-down inside to be truly available.

"Do you want to go grab ice cream?" he asked.

Stark interest in Rob's eyes. He hadn't moved, other than to stow his knitting in that sparkly bag.

Yes, she wanted to get ice cream. She wanted whipped cream and cherries, chocolate syrup and nuts, and maybe if she was lucky, sliced bananas. But his interest, more than anything else, was going to make her turn him down.

Because he deserved someone who was available.

He *deserved* someone better than her.

And that wasn't some self-pitying bullshit. Soph knew what she was, knew she was valuable as a human being. She worked hard, donated to charities, tried to do the best with what she was given.

But in this manner of abilities, in the skill of being open enough to be in a true relationship with someone, to be vulnerable and allow a man into her heart, she had only been given dredges.

She simply couldn't ever be what Rob—a good, kind man, who'd already survived too much grief—deserved.

So, she couldn't allow ties to form.

Distance. STAT.

Not looking at him, she lifted her bag, tucking it over her shoulder and pushing her chair back from the table.

"I'm sorry," she said. "But I actually have . . . a call I need to jump onto tonight."

Disappointment edging into his expression, that tiny scar at the corner of his mouth flashing bright white when his lips pressed flat. "Of course."

And, stupid woman that was, she found herself saying, "Maybe on Thursday?"

That mouth relaxed, becoming lush and kissable again, his eyes bright, and she knew she was in trouble. As dangerous as the charming, knitting man was, she so preferred to see him like this, rather than sad and disappointed and dragged through the wringer, and—

"Thursday it is," he said, standing. "I'll walk you to your car."

A shake of her head. "Oh, actually, I'm fine."

"Okay"—a shrug, a flash of that dimple—"you can walk me to mine."

She snorted.

He picked up his bag.

"Should I carry that for you, too?" she asked dryly.

His laughter filled the space, bouncing around happy and full and drawing the focus of Misty and the two other women who remained, the latter whose faces were all frozen in place.

Not Misty.

No, her expression was one of anticipation, of . . . expectation. Of hope.

Shit. Discomfort curled in Sophie's stomach, had her turning for the door, the *click-click* of her heels very loud in the now quiet space. She was going to have to seriously reconsider whether she was willing to be short if it meant not having to so noisily declare her exit from the room.

But *could* she give them up?

The height, the power?

Probably not.

Either way, she pushed open the door, slipped out onto the darkened street. Several restaurants were open, diners filling their outdoor tables, but many of the other shops were locked up tight, the streets having mostly rolled up.

Rob emerged behind her then stepped to her side, shortening his long gait to match her shorter one. "You really do wear those heels all the time."

"Yup."

"Armor," he said, his arm brushing hers lightly.

She kept walking, but everything inside her had arrested, stilling with the realization that he was right. *That* was why she couldn't give them up. Not just because they made her five-feet-nothing frame taller, made it so she could reach the top shelf in the grocery store or not have to climb onto the counter to get a mug out of the upper cabinets at her rental. Not because she felt sexy and strong in them.

But rather because, somehow, they'd become part of this image she'd created for herself.

Long lines and slender curves. Girly and put together.

Put. Together.

Because the chaos of her teen years had been anything but.

"I know something about armor," he said after they'd turned the corner and crossed the parking lot, pausing near her driver's side door.

She couldn't bring herself to ask *what* he knew.

Not with him so close, not with his scent surrounding her. Not with him being all . . . Rob-like.

God, she hardly knew the man, and yet she wanted him to touch her, wanted to touch *him,* to taste that tiny scar in the corner of his mouth, and she wanted—

Something she couldn't have.

Well, *that* certainly wasn't new.

"What is it?" he murmured, brushing his thumb over one corner of her mouth then the other, making her shiver. "What's made you smile?"

Soph shook her head. "It's nothing."

He lifted a brow, kept his eyes on hers.

And . . . she lost herself in the depths, found herself confiding in him, telling him the truth when with anyone else she would have avoided and prevaricated and given a funny, chipper, and/or pat answer.

Some part of her knew he'd see right through that.

Some part of her wanted to give him parts of her she'd never given to another man.

Alarm bells blared anew.

*Danger. Danger.*

Yeah, yeah. She knew all that, and still, Sophie told him anyway.

"I was just thinking it wasn't anything new to want something I couldn't have."

Stillness between them, every muscle in his body locking tight, freezing until he was like a statue. But only for a heartbeat. Then the statue breathed, then the man unstuck and leaned back against her car, arms crossed loosely over his chest. His hip was barely an inch from hers, his thigh perhaps even closer, though she didn't have time to fully process that before he asked, "What is it that you want?"

A quiet question.

A seemingly innocuous one.

Except when the answer was: I want *you!*

Her breathing was jagged, and she shook her head. "I need to go."

And she *would* have gone. Right then. Would have opened the door to her car, clambered into the driver's seat, and peeled out of the parking lot like she was the lead actress in the newest *Fast and Furious* film.

But right then, the stitches on her bag gave way. The strap slid from her shoulder, shooting down her arm. She scrambled for the unbroken piece of fabric, but it dropped down to her wrist, and she caught it with her fingertips, barely saving it from crashing to the ground but at the same time managing to dump all of her belongings onto the pavement.

Her wallet went one way, along with her lip gloss. Knitting needles and yarn went another. Her keys collided with his right boot. One sheet of the pattern clung to the top of the bag, while the other flew through the air, catching on the ocean breeze like a snowflake flurrying in the wind.

"Shit," she hissed, grabbing for it.

Rob beat her to it, snagging it out of the air and bending to carefully retrieve her knitting project, and she watched him move gently, ensuring it didn't slide off the needles as he tucked it back into her bag.

Then, as she was frozen, watching him tenderly stow her hardly begun scarf away, he bent again and picked up her wallet and lip gloss.

Those were also placed carefully inside her bag before he tugged the tote right from her fingers, snagged her keys, and unlocked her car. A soft *pop* as the door opened, and her breath caught when he bent around her to stow the bag on the passenger's seat.

She was still staring at him, watching him place it down, the canvas tote bright against the dark cloth of the seat, when he slowly straightened, ducking his head so as not to hit it on the car's frame.

Then he was there.

In front of her, *close* to her. Their bodies nearly touching as they stood in the narrow opening between the door and frame.

"What was it you wanted, but you couldn't have?" he asked, his voice barely above a whisper as he stroked the backs of his knuckles over her cheek, his other hand resting on the top of her car.

But she could hardly focus on the little details. Not when he was so near.

His touch.

His smell.

His *heat*.

The words bubbled within her, spilling out across her tongue before her brain managed to shake off the haze of her desire.

"I want you," she whispered.

His breath hitched, and she saw his hand that was resting on the top of the car tighten, his knuckles standing out in sharp relief, a soft curse on his lips.

Then he moved.

The knuckles lightly running along her cheek becoming a palm covering it, his body inches away became one that was flush to hers. Hard met soft, curves met muscles, and he aligned every part of hers with every part of his. But the movement that drew her focus the most intently was that of his mouth.

Drawing nearer.

Dipping closer.

Until it met hers.

# NINE
## WHEN THE SUN SETS

Rob

IT HAD BEEN a long time since he'd kissed a woman.

And he'd never kissed a woman who wasn't Carmella.

His love story with his late wife hadn't been riddled with breakups or on-agains/off-agains. They'd fallen, they'd stayed, they'd loved.

So, he'd never had anything to compare to.

And *this* . . . was different.

The same and different, and frightening and intense, and coming home and unique and . . . just fucking perfect, somehow all at the same time.

Sophie's lips were soft, pillowing against his as he brushed his mouth against hers, once, twice, three times, his fingers lightly clenching on her cheek, her skin like silk against his palm.

Then her lips parted, and the tip of her tongue brushed the seam of his lips—

And he stopped comparing. Stopped thinking.

His hand slid to her nape, angling her head back while his

other shifted from the top of the car to her hip, nudging her against the side of the vehicle, pressing into her until he could feel every glorious inch of her body.

Fire licked at his veins. His cock went rock-hard, desire blistering through him, razing him to the ground until it was just him with this woman.

Her tongue danced with his; her fingers gripped his shoulders, her body—

But fuck was it both luscious and lean, her breasts pressing against his chest, her ass filling his palm when he cupped her there and brought her somehow even closer. His other hand slid down, slipping from her hair, tracing along the outside of her arm, along her waist, down to that luscious hip. Except, it couldn't stay there, not with her moan vibrating along her tongue, drifting across his mouth, making his own groan of need echo through his throat. Fingers slipped under the hem of her sweater, felt the barest glimpse of silken skin, then faltered when they encountered a large, flat lump.

A scar.

Even as he was processing that and dismissing it—God knew, he had plenty of scars himself—Sophie's hands were coming up to his chest, shoving him away hard enough that he stumbled back into the door.

"I'm sorry," she said, eyes going wide, reaching out as if to steady him.

But not to reach *for* him.

No, that moment had passed.

He straightened even as she drew her hand back, clutching it to her as though she'd been burned.

Her eyes darted to the open door, to the seat inside, to her broken tote bag, to his chest, to *anywhere* but where he wanted —to his, so he could understand what emotion was bursting through, so he could help her, so he could—

Make her forget enough that she would kiss him again.

But she didn't look at him, and when her gaze drew progressively more panicked, he stepped back enough that she could easily get into the driver's seat.

Which she all but lurched into, collapsing into the seat in a heap, having to bend down and straighten one of the high heels she was always wearing. Yet, she still didn't look at him, merely pushed the button on the dashboard to start the engine.

And waited.

Still not looking, just waiting . . . for him to leave her alone.

So, he did.

Rob stepped back and shut the door, rounded the front of his truck, and watched as she screeched out of the parking lot.

The best damned kiss of his life.

And the woman responsible for it had all but ran screaming away.

---

HE FINISHED NAILING in the last bit of trim for the Fosters' new floor, and he had to admit that it looked pretty damned good.

They'd gone with a gray-stained, hand-scraped product, the matte finish making for the perfect beachy feel for this ocean-front cottage, and while he had to admit that the gray wouldn't have initially been his first choice, he'd bit his tongue—what the customer wanted and all that.

And had been proven decidedly wrong.

Bethany had clearly seen something he hadn't, he knew, filling in the last couple of nail holes with matching putty before straightening and snapping a picture with his cell.

Besides the flooring, he'd done all of the woodwork in this job—baseboard and crown molding, door frames and new window casings. He'd even constructed a built-in reading nook and bookshelves for the Fosters. And not to pat himself on the back, but the space looked damned good. So good, in fact, that he'd already gotten permission to put pictures of this job up on his website.

Now he was done, and he'd be moving on to the next client —that being a repair job for a deck and adding a new pergola to their back yard.

It'd be outside and positively chilly in the mornings.

But Rob didn't mind.

He liked working with his hands, loved that there was always something new to work on, even when he was dealing with subcontractors and invoices and delayed shipments of tile, like he and Misty were waiting for her bathroom remodel.

"This looks amazing," Bethany whispered, having come up behind him. "Is it all done?"

He nodded. "With the exception of a little cleanup I need to finish, I'd say you can get your reading nook filled with books in no time at all."

She smiled and hugged him. "Thank you," she said, stepping back and clapping her hands together. "I love this so much!"

"You're welcome." A beat. "Plus, I think you might have a career in designing ahead of you."

"Meh." She waved a hand. "I just watch too many home decorating shows."

He grinned as he bent and began picking up his tools. "Well, either way, everything you chose turned out great." He detached his nail gun, unplugged the compressor, and wound the air cord. "If you want, after I sweep, I can help you roll out your rug and bring the furniture in."

The delivery had come that morning as he was finishing up, one day late due to his birthday shenanigans.

"Oh, you don't have to do that," she said. "I'll just wait until Dave gets home."

"It's the least I can do after they had to stow everything in the hall because I fell behind schedule."

"Rob." Bethany's eyes went sad. "It's not your fault, especially—"

And that was a particular conversational track he didn't want to go down. "Actually, it would be doing me a favor," he interrupted. "The pictures on my website always look better when the furniture is in the rooms. Looks more finished."

She nibbled at her bottom lip. "Really?"

That was true. The next wasn't, since he had a waitlist of clients ten deep. "Plus, I can use all the help I can get. It's always hard to run a business in this economic climate."

"I suppose so," she said.

"Good." He hefted the compressor and hose, carefully slipping past her *and* the furniture stacked haphazardly in the hall, bringing both out to his truck, before returning with a broom and dustpan, cleaner and rags. One more trip outside to stow the nail gun, et al, and he got to cleaning.

Construction dust, no matter how careful he was, always seemed to get *everywhere*.

That tiny crack in the corner. On top of the mantle he hadn't even touched. Coating the doorknobs and everything in between.

So it was sometime later before everything sparkled and he was helping Bethany carry in the couch—gray cushions with peach and yellow throw pillows she arranged carefully as he went back out into the hall for the side tables. Then a mirror and he slipped out to his truck to retrieve his drill so he could hang it over the fireplace, along with a tryptic of paintings on the far wall. He plugged in lamps and rolled out a large rug while she fussed with knickknacks and stuffed the reading nook with books.

And by the time the sun was going down, the space was finished.

They both looked around the space before he smiled and nudged her lightly with his elbow. "You did good, kid."

"I'll have you know, I was only two years behind you in school."

"A lifetime," he deadpanned.

"Only in high school." She hugged him again. "Thank you so much, Rob." Then she snagged his cell and took a few pictures of the furnished space—which truthfully, *did* look better in pictures.

They talked about town gossip as she walked him to his truck. Apparently, the lacrosse team had some equipment stolen, and local businesses were stepping in to buy new items for the boys and girls.

"I didn't tell you this to get you to open your checkbook," Bethany said, when he'd reached into his glove box to do just that. "I'm supposed to be paying *you*."

"I know." But he wrote the check anyway.

Because this was Stoneybrook. Because they came together instead of pulling apart.

Plus, Bethany was the P.E. teacher at the high school, and he knew that if she didn't get enough funds to purchase the equipment, she would fund it herself. She worked hard, had scrimped and saved to afford the room remodel. Hell if he would allow her to scrimp and save even more, just because some asshat had stolen from innocent kids.

Yeah, no. That wasn't happening on his watch.

Later, after he'd waved off her offer of dinner, he got in his truck and started to drive home. Except . . . something drew him to the beach, to the parking lot that he and Carmella used to drive to in high school, make out in the dark as the sun set and the moon rose, and the windows fogged up.

Today, after years of avoiding their spot, he slid into the lot and sat in his car, watching the sky darken in front of him and . .
.

He didn't feel gut-wrenching, heart-stabbing pain.

Even though he couldn't hear Carmella's voice, even though she wasn't sitting next to him holding his hand, kissing his neck.

She was gone, and he was sad. He still missed her, still wanted his best friend.

But he wasn't wrecked.

Not any longer.

The moon rose, his stomach growled, and he drove home.

Alone, but perhaps for the first time in a long time, not totally empty.

# TEN
## AFTER THE KISS

Soph

SIGHING, she put down the script she was reading and pushed out her front door, feeling the salt air on her face, kissing her lips, tousling her hair, making her nipples bead against the cool silk of her pajamas.

Like a lover.

Like—

"Do *not* think his name," she muttered, reaching back into the house for the oversized hoodie she had taken to leaving on the hook there and slipping it over her head.

The sun was just peeking over the horizon in the distance— the sky still navy, a narrow strip of bright orange dancing along that edge, spreading upward.

She'd hardly slept the night before. Because of that man, because of . . .

The Kiss.

Yup. With capital letters.

Because she'd never been kissed like that before, never been held so gently and yet somehow still so passionately.

She'd *never* been on the receiving end of a kiss that had made her forget everything.

Who she was. Where she came from. What her past had made her.

Not until his fingers had brushed her back. Her scars. The reminder—

"Fuck," she whispered, closing the door behind her and yanking the sweatshirt's hood tightly over her face. Now the breeze wouldn't get in, wouldn't caress her face like the unnamed man she wished she could take as a lover.

It wouldn't remind her of everything that had been taken away from her before she'd even been able to give it.

Because what she wouldn't give to get to know that unnamed man—fuck, *fine*, she knew she was being ridiculous, so fine—*fine!*—she'd speak his name. Because what she wouldn't give to go on a date with someone like Rob. To get to know him. To have ice cream and chocolate syrup and cherries. To hold hands and go to the movies. To take midnight strolls on the beach.

But . . . it wouldn't ever be.

Sighing, she gave in and lifted her chin to the still dark sky, letting the air caress her skin, letting her remember the kiss and how it had made her feel. She needed to mark those memories, to hold them tight, to stow them away.

She needed to get used to having *just* memories.

Because that was all she and Rob would ever be. Soph knew that. She understood it was the way of the world. Which meant she needed to stop being morose and wishing things were different and get on with her vacation and living her life and learning how to knit that fucking scarf.

One kiss was all she'd ever have of Rob, and she needed to remember that.

To be content with it.

It was just . . . so fucking hard to actually *do* that after she'd spent the little bit of sleep she'd gotten dreaming about him, reliving his touch, the gentle insistence of his lips, the way his tongue had tangled with hers.

"Enough, Soph," she murmured. "Just *enough*."

With that, she took off down the beach, walking through the chilled sand. It seeped up between her toes, coarse and abrasive, and yet somehow still refreshing, as though it were scraping off an outer coating, exfoliating the dryness, leaving pinkened, softened skin in its wake. The air was slightly-sticky, moisture clinging to the currents, sending salt traveling along the shore. It clung to her face, her hair, leaving both feeling stiff.

Or maybe that was what was inside her.

A brittle stiffness. A careful bracing. One crack, one removed support, and she'd crumble to pieces.

*No.*

She wouldn't break.

She hadn't broken.

She *never* would.

A bird flew overhead, the sky having lightened enough during her musings for her to see its silhouette, and she didn't miss the symbolism. Flying high above the world. Alone in its journey.

By necessity.

*Surviving* alone.

By necessity.

Curling her legs beneath her, Sophie sank down into the sand, its coolness sweeping over her, soaking through her pajamas. But that cold was almost a comfort. It tempered the burning, the yearning, the *need* inside her until she finally felt more like herself.

Until she finally felt like that bird.

Flying free.

Untethered rather than just alone.

She scooped up handfuls of sand, letting the grains slip between her fingers, and cleared her mind, pushing any conscious thoughts to the back of her brain. Just sitting in the moment.

Just being thankful for how far she'd come.

That she even had a life to live.

Because the world went on even in the face of heartbreak and cruelty. People might send a condolence, an apology, even express outrage, demand change, but in the end, they would get on with their lives and forget.

Not because they were bad or heartless.

It was just human nature.

She'd lived enough life in her younger years to understand that some things didn't change, no matter the best intentions.

That was why she used her quiet time on the beach watching the sun slowly creeping up in the sky, the beach becoming brighter by the moment, to carefully rebuild the bricks around her heart, to lay them one by one so that she could shove down the darkness, the old pain, and . . . feel like herself again.

Not the shattered pieces she'd been after The Kiss.

Eventually, the sun was high enough that she knew she needed to walk back to her house, to put on real clothes instead of the worn pajamas she was currently sporting. So she pushed to her feet, dusted off her bottom, and headed back to her rental, listening to the waves crash against the shore as she did so.

Finn had been right to drag her butt here.

There was something soothing about this beach, even more so than the ones back in southern California. This wasn't quite as warm, and the clouds often clung to the sky overhead, but there was something peaceful, more settled about this tiny stretch of beach.

Fewer people, maybe.

Fewer cameras pointed in her direction, certainly.

Either way, despite her problems of the male persuasion, Soph felt more centered and rested than she had in years.

Probably not *too* surprising, considering she'd been working nonstop since that first film had hit big almost two years ago—between prepping for and then shooting four films back-to-back and squeezing in the press tours, she had been running on fumes before this month off.

Any place where she had privacy and could get some sleep would have brought the same result.

Probably.

Or not.

Because she wasn't sleeping well, and what little rest she'd managed had been marred by dreams of intense, swirling tiger's eyes belonging to he-who-must-not-be-named.

Yup, she was back to that again.

She paused at the bottom step that led up to the porch that looked out at the ocean, her front door set in the middle of two large glass windows, and groaned. "Get it together, Soph," she muttered. "Just forget it, so you can enjoy your vacation and—"

She choked on a scream when a shadow materialized into a man.

Coming toward her.

*Stalking* toward her.

No. God, no. Not again.

Stumbling back, her feet not working correctly, she tried to turn and run but somehow managed to trip over herself and land hard against the path that led to the front of the cottage. Her palms and knees burned as the concrete abraded her skin. Her lungs sawed, attempting to draw in air but not managing to get anything that resembled a full breath.

And the man moved closer.

She finally managed to get her knees under her, to push herself up onto her feet, turning away, even as the man spoke.

Well, maybe he'd been speaking the whole time, but she hadn't been able to hear him.

Not when she was like this—sweat sheening her body, her heart threatening to pound out of her chest, her pulse thrumming in her ears, making the words impossible to glean.

She skittered back, tried to run again.

Then tripped. Again.

Or *nearly* did, because the man's hand wrapped around her arm, catching her before she fell again.

His grip was gentle.

That was the first thing that processed.

Even stopping her from crashing onto her face, he still touched her with care, and *that* was the piece that had her ears beginning to work, the metaphorical soundproofing of her heartbeat slowing enough that she could hear again.

And *see* again.

See Rob.

Who was staring at her with those intense swirling eyes of golden and brown. Too intensely. Too clearly. He was watching her like he knew exactly what was traveling through her brain— the memories, the pain, the . . . shame.

Tearing her gaze away, she saw the drinks on the sand, dripping into darker puddles, the smell of pomegranate and spice mixing with the salt of the air.

Two carafes of tea.

*Spilled* tea.

She sighed, pulled against Rob's grip.

He didn't let her go, just swept her up into his arms and carried her up the stairs, across the porch, and into the house. It said a lot about this town that he barely paused to check if the door was locked—it wasn't, which probably said a lot about her state of mind that morning and also the influence of this little town because she *always* locked her doors—before he carried her into the house and down the hall, unerringly finding the bathroom and setting her on the counter.

"Let me see," he said softly, reaching for her hands.

"I'm fine," she whispered, holding them close to her chest.

He didn't argue, just bent to study her knees, gently peeling back the torn fabric and hissing out a breath when he saw what was beneath. "These need to be cleaned," he said, turning away and opening the linen closet, pulling out a small first aid kit. He set it next to her on the counter and unlocked the plastic tabs, removing the top and placing it to the side.

Bandages retrieved, along with some antiseptic pads. Both set next to her hip.

Then he spun around and disappeared.

Soph blinked at the hasty retreat then released a breath, her heart finally slowing to its normal rhythm as she figured he'd left her to clean her own cuts. Made sense. But just as that thought drifted to her mind, he reappeared, this time with a cup in his hand. He returned to the linen closet, grabbed a couple of towels, and then knelt in front of her.

Frozen in place, unnerved and exhausted as her adrenaline from the encounter faded, she just watched as he wrapped the towel below her knee then carefully poured water from the cup on her cuts.

She jumped at the first touch of that liquid, warm when she'd expected cold.

"Sorry," he murmured, moving even more slowly, more gently.

And all of a sudden, she came back into herself—fury and embarrassment mingling into an uncomfortable second skin.

"I'm not crazy," she hissed, trying to pull away. "Don't treat me like I am."

He didn't react, just tightened his grip, using the bare minimum of force to keep her in place.

Which only pissed her off more.

Especially when he set the cup aside and lightly dabbed her skin dry. Then in quick, practiced moves, he wiped the antiseptic and placed the bandages.

Only as he was moving to her second knee—and no, she wasn't looking too closely at the fact that she hadn't moved when he released her to shift positions—did he finally look up at her. "I'm sorry I startled you," he said more evenly than softly.

And her anger dissipated.

Because she hadn't been startled, so much as filled with bone-deep fear and panic. She'd been back in that place, back with that—

But this man didn't know that. He didn't know what he'd conjured.

How could he?

She could barely believe it herself. She'd spent so much time and effort shoving the memories away, pretending they didn't exist. But time in this town, in this place, with this man . . . and it was like the lid had begun to peel open, all the dark things from her past cropping up, all the feelings she'd spent so freaking long making sure she *didn't* feel were flooding in.

Probably, she should run screaming for the hills.

Probably, she should want to go back to the way her life was before. *How* she was before.

Content and closed down, happy in the slice she'd carved out for herself, knowing it was more than she'd ever expected.

Probably, she should leave. Right now.

But she wanted to feel . . . just for a little longer.

"No," she said, "it's not your fault."

"It is. I was the one who showed up unannounced." He

started cleaning her other knee, movements still as sure and gentle, even though the water was a little cooler now.

"I'm . . ." She closed her eyes, that lid peeling back further. But she forced it to halt in its progress, to not reveal any more. "Fine," she finished when she could speak without giving anything else away. "I just wasn't expecting anyone to be on my porch." He froze, and she opened her eyes to see him studying her. A shrug. A forced smile. "I startle easily."

More studying.

But he didn't call her on her lie.

And she decided it was time to change the subject. "How did you know where everything was?"

He lifted a brow.

"I mean the Band-Aids and towels and bathroom, for that matter," she said. "How did you know where they were?"

It was his turn to shrug. "I did the remodel on this house before it became a rental." Another when her brows lifted. "Small town, remember?"

"Oh, I remember."

He smiled at her and . . . God, it was so good that she wanted to take a picture so she could remember it forever. Or maybe bronze it and mount it on her wall at home. That tiny dimple winking at her. The way one side curled up slightly higher than the other. The small scar that demanded a kiss, for her to trace it with her tongue.

"Who hurt you?" he asked, and it was said so conversationally that for a moment, she didn't process the words.

Then she did.

Then . . . the shame came.

It had no right to. It shouldn't have any place in her life, not when her trauma wasn't her fault, not when she'd been the product of a shitty situation and an equally shitty family.

But she still felt it.

A heavy burden upon her shoulders, coloring every interaction.

That was why she buttoned everything down so tightly, locked it away with a dozen padlocks and heavy chains. Because she didn't want to feel this way any longer.

She hopped down from the counter, darting to the side when Rob made as though to grab her. "I don't need your help."

He leaned back against the door and crossed his arms. "Who hurt you?"

"It's none of your business," she muttered, turning on the faucet.

"Ah," he said. "So, there was someone."

"I—" She faltered. "I didn't say that."

"You didn't have to. It's in your eyes."

Soph was furious now—at him for presuming to think he had any right to know that, at *herself* because her past still had such a tight grip on her, at her family for all they'd done and because they were supposed to be the ones to protect her.

Instead, they'd thrown her right into the fire.

She shoved her hands under the stream, scrubbing them harder than she should in her fury, then hissing when the cuts opened again and the water got in deeper. Before she could pull them out from beneath the faucet, he was there, tugging her hands toward him, wrapping them in a towel, and gently drying them.

Unbidden, her eyes stung, and she looked away, determined not to meet his gaze.

He proved to be the more determined of their pair, turning her, peering down into her face, and she wondered what he saw there, if he could see beneath the brick wall and ferret out the secrets she hid beneath.

But if he did unearth them, nothing about his expression revealed his find.

"Who hurt you?" he asked again.

For a moment, she debated just telling him, just confessing it all then and there. He'd talked about his late wife, and she'd heard more from Shannon and the talk around town. So she certainly knew more about his pain than he did hers.

Her lips parted, the confession on the tip of her tongue.

Then panic smothered it.

His fingers brushed along her cheek, down her throat, coaxing her windblown hair behind her shoulders. "I am sorry for it," he whispered.

Her breath caught.

"For scaring you," he said, smoothing her hair back, "and for whatever was done to you."

Heart thudding in her chest, she swallowed hard, feeling the world tilt on its axis as her body drifted toward his. He leaned closer, and for a moment everything else fell away. His thumb, slightly calloused and work-worn, brushed along her bottom lip, sending a shiver down her spine as she inched closer.

He was going to kiss her.

She wanted nothing more.

Her mouth opened, tongue darting out to moisten her lips, and the moment stretched, drawing her in, filling her with yearning, with need, with desire.

*Closer.*

Two magnets at opposite poles being pulled together . . .

And then he straightened.

Physically distanced his body from hers.

Purposely dropped his gaze to her hands and instead of kissing her, he cleaned and bandaged her palms then drew her from the bathroom, nudging her into the bedroom, so she could change her clothes.

The door closed with a *click*, leaving her in the dimly lit space, and she found herself staring in the mirror, at a face that was both familiar and a stranger.

"Would it be so wrong for him to know?" she whispered to her reflection. Maybe they could find something in shared pain, maybe she didn't actually have to live like this any longer.

Maybe if she finally talked about it, the power would disappear and she'd . . .

She'd be able to have a real life, with a real, kind man like Rob.

"Maybe," she whispered, courage welling within her, making her consider, to *think*. She turned away from the mirror and quickly changed into jeans and a T-shirt, leaving her feet bare, not caring that her hair was tousled and a total mess around her shoulders. "Maybe I can. No," she said more firmly. "I *can* be different."

Hope bubbled up as she opened the door and hurried down the hall, her footsteps quiet.

"Rob?" She poked her head into the living room, found it empty.

Then the kitchen. Also empty.

The bathroom, the spare bedroom, and finally . . . the deck with the ocean in the distance, the mostly deserted beach. The sun steadily climbing above the horizon.

All empty of Rob.

That hope withered away.

She should have known.

# ELEVEN
## UNLOCKED DOORS

Rob

HE RETURNED to the cottage during his lunch break, unable to get Sophie's bleak expression out of his mind, and he found her on her deck, hat pulled low over her eyes, closed laptop propped on her stomach, and gorgeous body on display in an emerald green bikini.

After swallowing his tongue for several heartbeats, he managed to get it together enough to knock on the deck railing.

She tilted her hat up, those stormy gray-blue eyes locking onto him.

"Hi," he murmured, holding up the tea, round two, he'd brought. "Thought you could use a drink."

Silence. That gaze still locked on him.

"How are you?" he asked.

She sat up, tugging the silky robe thing she was wearing around her and belting it tightly around her waist. "Fine." A beat. "Thanks."

Then she tucked her computer under her arm, turned her

back on him, and walked into the house, the door clicking closed behind her.

Rob stood on her deck for a heartbeat then went after her.

One, because fuck that she'd walk away from him and freeze him out. They'd shared a moment and a kiss that had blistered his soul and . . . well, several more moments. She couldn't just walk away from him.

Well, of course, she *could* do that.

Especially considering she just had.

The lock *clicked.*

It was the *click* that did it.

The *click* that made his temper fray. He was trying to be nice. He'd brought her tea. He hadn't meant to scare her and had tried to make it right. Now, he was trying to make sure she was okay, and she just walked away?

What the hell?

Look, he got that she didn't owe him anything, and he wasn't one of those guys who couldn't take rejection—though having only dated one woman his entire life, a woman he'd then married, Rob couldn't pretend that he had a lot of experience in the endeavor.

But he did have experience being a friend, and as attracted as he was to Sophie, he knew what someone looked like when they needed a friend.

Soph was alone.

Was *used* to being alone, but he knew she deserved to have people around her who loved her and could appreciate her. He was just starting to know her, and he'd already seen so many wonderful things—the gift she'd brought him, the kindness in her eyes, calling Finn to come help him, treating his sister so kindly both while shopping and during the class.

She was a good person.

He knew that in his bones.

And for some dumbass reason, she thought she deserved to be alone.

Luckily for him, he knew where the spare key was hidden. In traditional Stoneybrook fashion, it was hidden under a flowerpot—the second one to the left of the door and filled with bright red and purple blooms. He lifted it, snagged the key from the little crevice beneath the pot, then moved to the front door, unlocking it and pushing inside before closing the door quietly behind him.

Sophie was in the kitchen, muttering to herself, cabinets opening and closing with *bangs*, something metal colliding with the counter, her feet smacking loudly against the tile floor.

He walked down the hall and into the kitchen.

God, she was beautiful, but not just the outside package, which, of course, was gorgeous. Glorious curves a man could grab on to, shining brown hair, a face that was pretty enough to grace film screens—and clearly had. But it was the emotions shining through her face that made him freeze in his tracks—fury and anguish, hope and fear, and then when she looked up and saw him standing in the hall, vulnerability.

But that was gone in an instant, replaced with anger, her chin lifting, her eyes narrowing. "How the fuck did you get in here?"

A shrug. "The spare key."

She cursed and turned her back on him for a second time. Then went back to her banging. "Great. You've shown you know all about this house, now go away."

He grinned, having seen Carmella in a mood like this often enough to not be upset or dissuaded or to take it personally. "I brought you something."

The metal teapot—the source of the *banging*—slammed down on the stovetop. "I don't care."

"But you'll *like* it," he cajoled.

She sighed and spun back to face him. "Wanna bet?"

He rounded the island, stepped between her and the stove. "Yes." Then he held up the tea he'd brought, close enough so the scent of it could waft under her nose. "I think you'll like it a whole lot."

Her lids fluttered shut as she inhaled, her moan soft but arrowing straight toward his dick.

Then she grabbed at the cup and started sucking down the tea.

"Better?" he asked.

Her blue-gray eyes flashed up, narrowed in his direction. "Why are you here?"

"I told you, I'd be back."

Confusion. "What are you talking about? You left me in the bedroom without a word."

"Um, I left a note." He pointed to the paper he'd left on the fridge, a pair of palm tree magnets holding it in place. "Told you, I had a job to get to but that I'd bring you a refill at lunchtime." Now he pointed at the clock. "It's lunchtime."

She set the cup down, walked over and read the note. Then spun back to face him, her cheeks bright pink. "I—uh—I—" She sighed, her chin dropping to her chest. "Can we start over?"

"No need to start over," he said, meaning it.

"I—" Another sigh. "I'm sorry."

"For what?"

She shoved her hair out of her face, came over to the counter, and picked up her tea, slugging back a long sip. "I'm sorry I'm in such a weird mood. I'm sorry I didn't thank you for tending to me this morning, and I'm sorry, I was such a bear just now. It's . . ." Her eyes slid closed. "Well, it's complicated, but no matter what's going on in my head, you don't deserve—" She peeled back her lids. "I'm on edge and took it out on you."

"What makes the edge better?"

"What?"

"What can we do to make you feel better?"

"I can—" She stopped, and he couldn't help but wonder if it were because she wasn't really sure how to answer that question, or she thought he was overstepping his boundaries.

Did she have the same need clawing at her?

Or did she want him to leave her alone? Perhaps she wanted what he did—to figure out why they were so drawn to one another. Why he'd dreamed of her. Why he'd been trying to figure out ways to see her when he had hardly given another woman a second look in years.

Why he was taking a fucking knitting class, complete with the pink sparkling bag.

Why he was here.

Why he was so fucking desperate to spend more time with her.

He brushed his fingers along her arm. "Will you come somewhere with me?"

She froze. "Where?"

Amusement curled through him, and he tugged at a lock of her hair. "Some place to clear your head."

"Why?"

He lifted a brow at the sharp question. "Because it's a good place to go and clear your head?"

"But you don't know me," she said. "Why would you care if my head is clear? Why would you care about me at all?"

Shifting a little closer, he tucked that lock of her hair behind her ear. It felt like silk, and he wanted nothing more than to keep rubbing it between his fingers, to continue stroking it, to feel it running over his naked skin. But that wasn't prudent for his cause, nor his thoughts. Because part of him thought he should be too terrified of being hurt to pursue this draw, that he should be running in the other direction.

The rest of him knew he'd only felt this way once in his life before, knew this was too precious a gift to give up.

It should be cherished and protected and nourished.

But she was tetchy with him just asking her to ice cream, so it wasn't like he could tell her that the moment he'd seen her stepping out of her car in those high, high heels and that tight skirt, the moment she'd told him off for being an idiot wandering into the street in the middle of the night, his heart had stuttered and frozen.

Then it had taken notice.

And when he'd sobered up, he recognized that notice for what it was.

*Forever.*

He just had to convince Sophie of that.

And based on her darting eyes, the way she was clutching the sleeves of her cover-up, her arms tightly crossed over her body, mentioning the fact that he wanted to keep this woman forever wasn't going to go over very well.

Yeah, no.

Instead, he turned the tables on her. "Why did you care enough to bring me a birthday present?"

"I—uh—" She faltered, her gaze meeting his then doing more of that darting to and fro. Then determination gathered at the edges of her eyes, and her chin came up. "I wanted to, okay?" Her shoulders straightened.

He bit back a grin. "Okay with me." A beat. "So long as you know that it's the same for me."

She froze. "I—what?"

"Come with me," he murmured. "Just trust me?"

Silence. Long and drawn out and tense.

"Soph," he whispered, lacing their fingers together and bringing her hand up to his mouth to press a light kiss to the back of it. "I have a rare afternoon off. Will you come with me?"

Her hand shook, but he just stroked it lightly. "I promise I'm not a serial killer."

She gave him a shaky smile. "That's what a serial killer would say."

And he knew he had her.

"I need to get changed," she whispered, backing up a step and nodding toward the bedroom.

Yup, he definitely had her.

He nodded, released her hand.

White teeth pressing into a plump bottom lip.

"Go ahead," he murmured, nudging her toward the hall.

She took two more steps, faltered, and turned back. "I—" Her words stalled.

"Jeans, sneakers, and layers in case you get cold."

"I—" A sharp shake of her head. "How did you know?"

"I was married," he said and winked, the memory more bittersweet than painful. "And I was trained well. No heels today, sweetheart."

Her lips parted then she smiled.

And it took his fucking breath away.

And . . . it told him he was on the right path.

# TWELVE
## THESE HEELS WERE MADE FOR WALKING

Soph

SHE WAS WEARING HEELS.

Heeled sneakers that had made Rob's lips turn up at the corners, given her a glimpse of that dimple. But she couldn't completely give up her heels, not when part of her felt that she needed her armor.

Not when she wanted to look tall and skinny and pretty.

And no, she wasn't examining *that* feeling too closely.

Especially when Rob hadn't commented on the pseudo-heels, instead taking her hand and leading out the front door, along the path, and to his truck. It was remarkably clean inside, not even the odd fast-food wrapper or soda can. The outside was also clean, even though there were a few scratches along the bed of the truck, presumably from him carrying tools or lumber in the back.

It was a working truck, none of the pretty boy, my-dick-is-bigger-than-yours nonsense she'd seen in L.A.

"Here." He reached over and started to buckle her seat belt, making her inhale sharply and getting a nose full of his scent.

Intoxicating.

Sawdust and salt. Spice and man. She wanted to wrap her arms around him and bury her face in his neck, to inhale again and again until his smell was imprinted on her soul.

*Click.*

She blinked, pressed her head back against the seat back.

"Okay?" he whispered, straightening slightly, until his face was directly in front of hers, until that tiny scar was mere millimeters away from her tongue, until . . .

Fuck it.

She gave in, wrapped her arms around those broad shoulders, and let her mouth fall to his.

Heat.

It roared over her like a forest fire, burning through her, incinerating her reservations, making her forget that she didn't feel—wasn't *supposed* to feel. The touch of his tongue on her lips had sensation pouring through her, her nerves shooting sparks, her thighs widening to allow him closer.

And when that slightly roughened palm cupped her cheek, angling her head so he could more easily devour her, she forgot all about what she was supposed to and not supposed to do.

She just felt. And acted. And . . . fucking *felt*.

He groaned, a deep, rasping sound that had her pussy clenching, her hands gripping his shoulders tighter, drawing him even closer.

A warm hand sliding up her side, cupping her breast through the fabric of her T-shirt.

She cried out, pushed into the touch.

But then the kiss slowed, his tongue retreating into his own mouth, his palm sliding away, sliding off.

And then he was pulling away.

Her fingers gripped his T-shirt, held him close for one more moment.

The invitation tumbled off her tongue. "We can go inside—"

His palm returned to her cheek. "Not today, Tempest." He smoothed her hair back, still unruly from the sea air, but his eyes were hot, and she should be the one calling him tempting . . . or tempest or whatever he'd said.

Her pulse was still pounding in her ears, her breathing unsteady.

She couldn't be sure what he'd called her.

What she *could* be sure of was that she wanted to go back to kissing him.

A rumbled curse, his fingers contracting on her cheek, but then he straightened abruptly, and a second later, he was out of the car, closing her door softly and rounding the hood to get into the driver's side.

He sat down, the cab bouncing lightly.

His gaze met hers.

Her lips parted.

He groaned, reached for her. "Fuck it, just one more."

She couldn't agree more.

She reached for him, too.

---

HER FEET WERE KILLING HER.

But she'd decided on the heels, so she'd suck up her discomfort. It was her own dumbass insecurity that had her needing to look long and lean and sexy, even though she knew she would never be one hundred percent secure with herself.

The industry she worked in was tough on a woman's confidence.

But her insecurity had been seeded well before a movie exec had asked—no, wait, merely *suggested*—that she might feel healthier if she were only fifteen pounds lighter. Oh, no, her insecurity had a long history, tangled with the other painful memories, until she felt as though her life was like a patch of wild blackberry she'd once accidentally stumbled into.

Long green vines, some thick, some thin, and all with thorns that had cut through the cotton of her shirt, pricked her skin through the denim of her jeans.

Pain—sometimes big and sometimes small, but always, *always* there.

So much easier to slap a lid on it and pretend it didn't exist.

But out here . . . with the cool air sliding against the bare skin of her arms just like in Stoneybrook, it was hard to pretend those long covered-up thorns didn't actually exist. Also, yes, she was glad that Rob had suggested layers because it hadn't been long before she'd stripped off her sweatshirt.

Maybe it was because here she wasn't surrounded by people every day—on photoshoots with hair and makeup people, on set with the same, plus directors and producers, at home with her assistant or publicist or agent, planning the next steps.

Here the background noise was gone.

Her eyes strayed to Rob's back, to the sweat beginning to soak through his T-shirt, outlining the muscles beneath, making her stomach flutter, her thighs tremble, her pussy . . . well, that had been on high alert for a while now, but after the kisses in his truck, it was at DEFCON 1. And she was beginning to think that maybe fate had provided her an opportunity, that the sliver of hope she'd had that morning actually *was* warranted.

That perhaps her past wasn't so much of a burden as she'd always thought.

She knew what the *real* burden was.

And it was this hill.

Ha.

Truthfully, it wasn't all bad, a narrow trail that required them to walk one foot after another and was only slightly terrifying if she looked down the hill, which shouldn't actually be called a hill, but rather be given categorization as a cliff, if she had anything to say about it.

The cliff/hill aside, it was warmer here than at the beach, though not unpleasant. There were enough trees around to provide shade, and honestly, not much could compare to the humid, oppressive heat of the Midwest town she'd grown up in.

This was damp and fresh smelling.

Quiet except for their footsteps and the sounds of nature—the whistling of the wind, the rustling of the leaves, the occasional crack of a branch.

The semi-often curse coming out of her mouth.

Like right then. When she tripped.

Again.

Rob halted and turned back, just like he had each time she'd almost stumbled to the ground.

And just like each time before, his palms found her shoulders, steadied her.

Only *this* time, he shifted the small pack he was carrying to his front, turned to give her his back, shaped his arms like hooks, and said, "Hop on."

"Um, what?"

A smile over his shoulder that made her suck in a rapid breath. "*Um*, hop on, Tempest, we're almost to the top."

"I can make it."

Still smiling. "That, I know. But throw me a bone here. I can't be responsible for the death of Hollywood's newest *It Girl*"—puppy dog eyes—"think of what it'll do to my sister. She loves you."

Soph stepped closer. "I don't think your sister has recognized me."

"Oh, no," Rob told her, waiting, his arms—and shoulders—at the ready. "She's recognized you, and she *looooves* you in that film you did with Finn. We're all just too cool here in Stoney-brook to bother you."

"Or jaded."

He straightened, turned to face her. "Not jaded."

"Then what?"

"Intoxicated." He ran a finger along her collarbone and dipped it into his mouth.

A strangled sound emerged from her lips.

"Because you taste good," he said. A light bop to her nose. "But not jaded. Just . . . desensitized to fame and stardom." He bent slightly, until their gazes were level, until she felt her pulse pick up at the intensity of his expression. "And I see you." A beat. "The *real* you underneath the veneer."

She fucking hoped not.

Because underneath that veneer was some scary shit.

"Now," he said, spinning back around, arms assuming his previous position. "Hop on."

Soph looked from Rob to the trail to her shoes and back to Rob.

Who was watching her, patience on his face.

And she figured . . . what the hell?

She placed her hands on his shoulders, bent her knees as though to jump—

"*Oh!*"

One second her feet were on the ground, the next she was in the air, warm arms clamped under her thighs—yum!—and she was clutching to his shoulders, holding on tightly. His heat surrounded her, along with his scent, and for a minute her head spun with the utter deliciousness of it.

Then he began moving—and at a much faster clip than she'd been managing.

He should be huffing and puffing as he hauled her ass up the cliffside, up the winding trail, but he wasn't. Instead, he was carrying her as though she weighed nothing.

"I should have thought of this long ago," she said, relaxing into the hold. "Before the blisters."

His shoulders went stiff beneath her and in the next moment, she found herself seated on a rock on the side of the trail, her foot in his lap as he knelt in front of her. "Blisters?" he exclaimed. "Let me see."

"I'm fine—"

But then her shoe was off, along with her sock, and before she had a moment to worry about the state of her feet when it came to the sweat and smell, his face was all up in there.

All up in there.

"Damn." He cursed. "You *do* have blisters."

"It's my fault," she said, reaching for her sock. "I should have picked my running shoes."

"Or," he muttered. "I should have not taken you up here in these shoes." He reached into the pocket of his backpack and pulled out a small first aid kit, then for the second time in a day, he bandaged her boo-boos.

"I can do it."

He ignored her, just gently put padding over the blister before stripping off her other shoe and sock.

Then glaring down at those blisters and repeating the process.

Geez. She was a train wreck, a hot mess, a total dumpster fire.

She couldn't even hike one trail without making it a big thing, without ruining this nice man's afternoon off.

"I'm sorry," she whispered.

"Don't apologize," he growled.

"But—"

He put away the garbage. "This is on me. I didn't tell you where we were going. I should have made you change or taken you somewhere else or—"

His hands were shaking, though still gentle as he stroked them over her abused feet, and she covered them, holding them in place. "Why are you so upset?"

"Because . . ." He sighed. "I'm supposed to be taking care of you."

For some reason, the grumble made her grin. "And if I say I don't *need* taking care of?" she asked archly.

His eyes flashed. "I'd say you'd—" He broke off, finished with the Band-Aids, and stowed the kit away. His voice was more controlled when he said, "I'd say you're not going to get me to bite on that question."

She giggled. "Maybe you're right."

"No maybe about it," he said or rather grumbled again. Warm fingers slid on her sock, carefully tied her shoe. "Come on." Then he bent again, so she could clamber onto his back.

Soph hesitated.

He lifted a brow.

She lifted hers.

"We're almost to the top," he coaxed.

"Hmm." But she was already reaching for him, fingers itching to stroke that broad back again, to be pressed against him.

He snagged her legs, but she snagged the backpack. *Ha.*

"Sophie," he warned.

"You carry me," she said. "I carry it."

Which obviously didn't make sense. He was carrying her, would feel the extra weight whether it was on her shoulders or his. But slipping the backpack onto hers made her feel like she was at least doing *something*.

He sighed but didn't argue further.

Instead, he hefted her higher, cupped her thighs a bit more snuggly, then began walking back up the trail.

And when he got them both to the top, she knew it had been worth the blisters.

# THIRTEEN
## ON A CLIFF

Rob

HE PLACED her lightly on her feet, her sharp inhale matching his.

He'd come up here so often that he could practically draw it from memory (if he'd had any skill at drawing, that was), but since he didn't, he just needed to rely on the images in his brain.

The ones in his phone had never seemed to capture the magic, so he'd stopped trying.

Now, when he had a spare afternoon, he tried his best to make it up here.

But it had been a long while since he'd managed.

"This is beautiful," she whispered, walking to the edge of the small clearing. Well, limping to the edge and making him feel guilty all over again for having let her wear those dumb shoes.

He should have stopped her.

It was just . . . she'd looked so playful and mischievous, and he hadn't been able to burst her bubble. Not to mention they'd made her ass look—

Chef's kiss.

Total chef's kiss.

His heart pulsed.

Because that was a saying he'd gotten from Carmella, and it hurt both good and bad.

Soph came close, her shoulder brushing his. "Did you bring your wife here?"

He shook his head. "No, Carmella was a beach addict, through and through." He smiled. "She preferred flip-flops and bare feet to any other sort of shoe."

"A girl who knew what she wanted."

"Yes." He took her hand, led her back to the edge, drawing them both down so they could rest their backs against a boulder, their legs hanging over the edge. "She definitely knew what she wanted."

Silence fell between them for a long time.

His gaze was on the scenery, absorbing the peace, the smells, the . . . feeling of calm, of being small in a big world that always came over him in this place.

"Will you tell me more about her?"

He glanced down to see that Soph was holding herself carefully, as though she were bracing herself for rejection. But he couldn't reject this woman with the shadows in her eyes, who also wore such strong armor that he'd hardly had a glimpse of what was beneath. "She was my best friend," he said simply. "We were together as friends and then partners for so long that I almost didn't know how to be myself without her. We were like two of those trees planted too close, trunks intertwining as they grew instead of being separate beings. And she was always so . . . big."

Sophie took his hand. "Big how?"

Rob smiled. "She had a big personality, could light up a room, and *fuck,* but she could talk." A laugh. "But she could take over, too, dominate a conversation, never back down from a fight, and *boom*"—another laugh—"her temper was something to behold."

"I think I would have liked her," Soph murmured.

"I know you would have." He ran his fingers over her palm, the inside of her wrist. "Everyone did."

"And then she was gone."

A nod. "And then I had to find a way to live again."

"I bet that was . . . well, hard seems like such an inadequate word."

He smoothed back her hair. "I bet you know something about having to do the same."

She went still. Like a statue. Like the boulder they were braced against.

And he thought he'd blown it, that he'd pushed when he should have just given, should have shown patience.

Then she slumped down, shifting her hips to the side as she rested her head on his lap.

It was his turn to freeze, to go perfectly still.

She was facing away from him, her legs curled almost like a question mark, her shoulder against the ground, her head laid across his thigh.

"Yes," she whispered. "Yes, I have."

He thought she was going to leave it at that, and the admission was enough. God, he knew it was so much more than anything he deserved. But then she sighed, and then she began talking.

And *then* his heart broke for her.

"My real name isn't Sophie," she whispered. "It's Candace."

"That's pretty, too."

A nod. "It is, and I liked my name. For a while, anyway. I used to watch old episodes of *Full House* and loved that my

name was the same as the actor who played my favorite character." She glanced back at him. "DJ was awesome."

He smiled, gave in to the urge to run his fingers through her
hair.

She looked out at the rise in the distance, the acres and acres
of green trees that filled the basin they were sitting above. But
she didn't stop him from touching her. Instead, she was quiet
again, and he had the sense that she was sorting her thoughts,
figuring out how much to tell him, or perhaps *how* to tell him.

"I didn't change my name because I didn't like it, or because
I wanted to change it to become more Hollywood." Her top
shoulder rose and fell on a sigh. "I changed it—no, I was forced
to change it when I went into protection."

He frowned.

A bead of moisture dripped onto his hand and for a second,
he thought it was from the trees overhead. Then he realized his
thigh was damp as well. She was crying. Because he'd forced her
to share something.

Fuck.

He slid his hands beneath her, pulled her up against him,
and held her tight. "Don't tell me," he whispered. "You don't
need to tell me, not when it's hurting you."

Twin tracks of tears marring that beautiful face, making her
gray-blue eyes look like the shining waves of the deep ocean.
But instead of nodding or agreeing with him, she smiled slightly
and touched his cheek. "You're a good man, you know that?"

Another tear fell.

"Soph," he groaned. She was killing him. He'd hardly begun
to know this woman, and yet the sight of her in pain absolutely
undid him.

"I've always thought that my past would make it so that
anyone with any good in them would turn away, would look at
me with disgust." She swallowed, pressed a finger to his lips

when he began to protest. "But I've never felt about another person the way I feel about you. I hardly know you, and yet"— she dashed away the tears—"I *know* you. I know you loved your wife and that you like tea. I know you must have let Misty teach you how to knit long ago, based on your skills displayed during class. I know that your sister looked at you with real love in her eyes and not mere sisterly affection. I know that you've been a good friend to Finn and Shannon because both of them have no shortage of nice things to say about you. Not to mention Rylie." Her lips quirked. "And I know that you've touched me gently, helped me just because you're a decent person, and . . . I know I want to bring you close, to let you in, to not just be this pretty posterboard of emotions and feelings but without any real depth, that I projected to the world."

She paused, chest heaving, pulse pounding against where his hand rested on her nape.

Then she straightened, said, "I have spent so much of my life locking my feelings down, determined not to feel, not to remember. It was *easy* to act, easy to channel my emotions purely into a script, because it wasn't *me*. I could keep thinking I was ice and untouchable and completely neutral because it was the scripts, the characters, the lines I'd memorize, and not me." Her shoulders slumped. "But it was *always* me. I'm not a computer to be programed, those emotions had to come from somewhere. It was just safer for me to pretend that they weren't from me. Because if they *were* from me, then I'd have to remember what it felt like to—" Her throat worked then her voice lightened. "Anyway, but then I came here, and I almost ran you over, and it was like all of a sudden I could *feel*."

He kissed the finger pressed to his mouth, gently peeled it away. "That's my specialty."

Her eyes danced with amusement. "Nearly getting run over."

"Exactly." A shrug. "Well, that, and creating all sorts of annoying emotions."

She laughed. "Okay, that's definitely true." A giggle. "It's like a couple of days with you in this town, and everything I thought I knew had gone by the wayside."

"Must be something in the water."

Warm eyes, a soft hand on his cheek. "No, it's *you*."

And then she kissed him.

# FOURTEEN
## THE DARK

Soph

SHE COULD KISS this man for the rest of her life, just spend an eternity sipping at his mouth, stroking her tongue along his, reveling in the feel of his hands running over her body.

But she needed to finish her story.

Pushing lightly on his chest, she pulled her lips from his and dropped her forehead to his chest, her breath coming in rapid puffs, desire making her skin feel too tight to fit over her skeleton.

He groaned, his fingers slipping under her T-shirt and skating along the skin of her back.

That touch cleared her mind.

Tight skin. Painful skin. Scars that would never go away.

"Let me go," she said, careful to keep her voice neutral, especially when she wanted to shove him away, to scream at him to release her *that instant.*

She didn't show anyone her back.

Not anyone. Not to a lover. Not in a film.

She'd had it written into her contract for a body double, never wore backless dresses.

Because of the scars.

Not because she was ashamed of them, *per se*, but because of what they represented. *Who* they represented.

Rob, to his credit, immediately released her, scooting back to give her space.

"It's not you," she whispered. "It's just—"

Then she shored up every last bit of courage she possessed and lifted the back of her shirt, revealing the last of her insecurities. She'd leave them all up on this mountain—her shame of the scars, the armor she'd used to close herself off from the world, the pain of her past.

Over.

Done.

Peeling that lid fully off and tossing the fucker over the cliff.

"These," she said.

His fingers brushed the skin of her back, rippled and hardened, still pink and abused-looking even all these years later. "You're still beautiful. I don't care about these."

"I don't either." She put up her hand when he started to reply. "I don't care that I have them," she said. "I care what they remind me of, what was taken from me." Teeth pressing into her bottom lip. "And what I'll never get back."

Fingers lacing through hers, tugging her to his side, his other hand rubbing up and down her spine. "What won't you get back, sweetheart?"

So. Many. Things.

But things he would only begin to understand if she told him about them. "When I was thirteen, I realized the truth about what my family was involved in." She inhaled, released a shaky breath. "Drugs. Violence. Prostitution rings. I always just thought I was lucky growing up. We lived in a big house. My dad worked from home a lot. My mom was beautiful and always dressed in the absolute latest fashion." A shrug. "I had any toy you could think of, nice clothes, professional haircuts. It was luxurious, and I was absolutely spoiled. I didn't want for anything. The moment it was mentioned, or I saw a commercial or a printed ad for something I might want, someone went out and bought it for me. Same with meals. We had a full-time chef at the house, and he would cook anything I wanted." Her lips pressed flat, released. "I never cleaned a room, a toilet, put a dish in the sink. I was indulged to the extreme."

"What happened?"

"My father got into some financial trouble—a drug deal went wrong, and he needed capital or the entire operation would collapse." She forced herself to hold his stare, remembering how quickly everything had changed, how the staff had gone, her nice things taken away. How he'd— "Turned out, *I* was the capital."

Rob's eyes darkened, but he didn't interrupt, just held her hand, his thumb rubbing lightly on her palm, and let her talk.

"It sounds like a bad movie," she whispered. "Like some role I would never *ever* agree to take on." She forced the words out through numb lips. "But the truth, the horrible, shattering truth is that my father sold off my virginity to the highest bidder."

Rob cursed, his hand clenching around hers.

But still, he didn't speak.

Which meant she did. "It turned out that he was under investigation by the FBI. They had been the ones to make that deal go awry, that had forced him to . . . well, find other ways to finance his operation. No." She shook herself. "*No.* It's not their fault, not really. The truth is he used and discarded me like he did the rest of the women in his life."

"Soph."

"I know. I *know*," she whispered. "But it turned out, the FBI had shit timing. They raided the house." Her shoulders had crept up around her ears. She forced them to relax. "After I'd been sent off for my night with the buyer. And during the raid, my parents didn't go quietly like they expected. Instead, they went down guns blazing, Hollywood shoot-out style with the SWAT teams, taking out the people who were supposed to retrieve me and leaving me with the man who'd—" Her eyes closed, the darkness and pain and fear so deeply entrenched that, for several minutes, it took every bit of her concentration to just breathe.

"How long?" he asked softly.

"What?" she whispered.

"How long were you there?"

She winced.

He cursed.

"But eventually, the task force uncovered the payment, traced it back to the man who'd purchased me." A beat. "They got me out, brought me to the hospital, and eventually into protection. I became a key witness in their case. Not that they needed me," she added. "As these things are wont to happen, before the actual trial, the man who'd bought me, who'd raped and abused and imprisoned me was found dead in his cell of a suspected suicide." She tugged at the hem of her T-shirt, straightening it. "But the agent who took me under his wing, who first looked at me when I was healing mentally and physically, suggested that was improbable. More likely, he said, the other prisoners had caught wind of his affinity for young kids and they'd punished him as they saw fit."

"Good," Rob said, the word sounding like broken glass cutting its way up his throat.

"I don't disagree with you," she told him. "But it left me in a pickle. I wasn't any use to the FBI anymore, my protection detail ran out, and I had no family alive left to take me."

His breath caught.

She squeezed his arm, the strong muscles beneath his skin feeling like absolute steel. "The agent who found me took me in, adopted me." Her lips turned up. "I became part of the Jacksons —a self-described nosy, pushy family who folded me into their crew and sheltered me under their respective wings, just as their father had in the hospital. In one day, I became a distant cousin whose parents died in a car accident and was adopted by Ben, rather than a damaged drug lord's daughter who barely knew how to make a peanut butter sandwich, let alone how to be on her own in the world."

She ran her fingers up and down the tanned skin of that forearm, tracing the occasional scar, feeling the slightly coarse hair against her palm. "My story, as outlandish as it is, has a happy ending. I got to be part of a good family, and my chosen career means I can take care of them like they once took care of me. It's just . . ."

His hand traced up and down her arm, but he waited for her to get her thoughts together.

"They treated me like one of them. They *loved* me. But I've always kept this barrier between me and them, part of me thinking that they would eventually look at me and realize I wasn't . . . worthy, I guess." She sighed, avoided his gaze when he sucked in a breath. "I know that's bullshit. *Logically,* I know that. But for many years after they adopted me, I did everything I could to test them, to test the bond between us. And it didn't matter what I threw at them, that I refused to go to therapy when I moved in with them, and then only begrudgingly attended the sessions when they forced me to." She made a face. "I certainly didn't get nearly what I should have out of them. And they *didn't* care that I fought them, that I kept them at arm's length, refused to let them in." Swallowing hard, she said, "They didn't care that I left for L.A. as soon as I could, that I hardly returned home for years, that I slept with more people than I should have because I didn't value my body, didn't value *myself* after what had happened to me. They didn't care about any of that. Instead, they were *proud* of me."

She cleared her throat.

Rob laced his fingers with hers. "You survived. That is a big thing to be proud of."

"That's something Ben would say." A slow breath. "And felt. Because they were so freaking proud when I landed the cheese commercial, even more so when I was in my first movie and the part got left on the editing room floor. They were proud of me for building a life, even though I wasn't proud of myself. I just wish I'd had it in me to be proud of myself, too. But it didn't matter. I did survive. I did make that life." She forced a smile. "See? Happy ending. Not every kid in my situation gets to be with a family who loves her unconditionally."

But her shame wasn't so easy to shed. It had taken years for her to understand that she didn't need to use sex to fill that void in her, to make her feel *something,* years to understand that all the random encounters with strangers—none of whom she'd ever let touch her back, to be so close to the thing that made her most vulnerable—were hurting her instead of making the past disappear.

Thankfully, she'd come out of that time without an STI, without an unplanned pregnancy, and with some measure of self-worth that had convinced her that fucking around wasn't the way.

She'd taken a time out from intimacy, from sex, had given herself an opportunity to make it not about hurting herself.

Instead of trying to fill that abyss with unhealthy, harmful interactions, she'd refocused, redoubled her efforts on her career.

And she'd landed the role with Finn.

That was what she meant about the happy ending. She was lucky, and she knew it, and with that, she ran out of steam, her heart thudding, sweat prickling on her forehead.

She'd told him everything.

Now, would he make her biggest fear come true?

Would he know the truth, believe it, look closely, and would he leave? Oh, he might walk her down the hillside, drive her back to her rental because he was a good man, but he'd drop her off and never come back and—

"Soph," he whispered hoarsely.

She managed to meet his gaze.

"Will you let me—" He broke off, reached for her. "Come here," he growled, pulling her onto his lap, wrapping his arms tightly around her. "Just . . . please, just let me hold you."

She didn't fight being cuddled against that muscled chest, held by those strong arms. Because it was Rob, and it felt incredible to be so close to him, embraced so tightly, hugged like she was wonderful and precious and not fragile exactly, but like she was something valuable and cherished.

"Fuck, Sophie," he said, burying his face in her neck.

Hot breath puffed on her throat, his pulse thrummed against her skin, and his hands were careful, but his hold was inescapable.

Good thing she didn't want to escape.

Good thing she wanted this man to hold her forever.

"I'm so sorry that happened to you." He released her enough to meet her eyes. "I want to murder your father, to kill the man—no, to fucking *shred* the man who thought that it was okay to buy you, to rape you, to hurt you, even though they're dead already. I want—"

His words faltered, and he just buried his face against her, just held her tight, all over again.

It took a long time for his breathing to slow, for him to not hold her quite as tight.

Eventually, though, he straightened, loosened his grip, and leaned back. "I'm sure you've been told this before," he said. "But it's not your fault. None of it. What happened to you is fucking unforgivable, and"—his fingers came to her chin, clasped it lightly between pointer and thumb—"I am so fucking proud of you for surviving that, for somehow becoming a functional adult. I cannot believe how strong you are. It just . . . I am in absolute awe of your strength."

Her pulse had long since slowed, an edgy sort of tension filling her, slowly freezing her heart, her limbs, her entire body until she felt like some sort of statue—granite like the boulder behind her.

But his words . . . his words made her *feel.*

"I don't see myself that way," she whispered. "I feel so weak all the time, so closed down and incomplete, like something was broken and I'll never be normal again."

"But something *was* broken," he said, running his fingers through her hair. She loved when he did that, almost haphazardly caressing, only half paying attention as he gently untangled the long unruly locks. "I don't mean that in a bad way. Just that something was stolen from you, and a life you thought was one thing turned out to be completely different. Your expectations were shattered and no matter how you tried to piece the shards of your life back together, it will never feel exactly the same again." His hands moved to her arms, rubbing up and down lightly. "But that doesn't mean you can't build something better, something more."

"Rob." Her voice broke. "I haven't even been able to talk about this before."

"And you think that just because it took you a long time to take the first step that it's not of worth?"

"I—" Well, put it that way. "No."

He smiled. "Good," he said, cupping her cheek. "Because as a person who just took a first step into sharing his own feelings, his own hurt—even though it cannot begin to compare with what you have been through—I can tell you that the first step is the absolute worst."

"Yeah?"

"Yeah." A kiss to her lips—short, firm, dizzying, and *wonderful*.

"Does that mean the rest of it will be easy?" she asked when they broke apart.

He rested his forehead against hers, chuckled. "Fuck, no."

Laughter bubbled up in her throat, and she found herself throwing her arms around him, hugging him close. He returned the favor, and they stayed in that embrace, chuckling and holding on tight for a long time.

And somehow, after she had just exposed her deepest, darkest hurts, she was laughing.

On a cliffside.

With a wonderful man running his fingers through her hair.

# FIFTEEN
## THE GREAT DEBATE

Rob

"YOU ABSOLUTELY CANNOT BE SERIOUS," he said, sitting back in the chair on Sophie's porch cradling his mug of tea and moving his gaze from the shoreline—in which he couldn't see anything anyway—and turning it to the far more interesting woman next to him.

The delicate features of her face were partly shadowed in the moonlight, but she was somehow even more beautiful than he'd realized.

Steel tempered in fire.

She crossed her arms and glared back at him. "I am *certainly* serious. As thus, I can confidently say that *Star Trek* is far superior to *Star Wars*."

"That is blasphemy."

One brow lifted. "The Enterprise."

"Is that supposed to be evidence for *Star Trek*'s superiority?"

She just shrugged.

"Because if it is, then I've misjudged you greatly."

"Oh?" she asked archly, sipping from her mug of tea.

"Yes," he said. "I only have to say Millennium Falcon to give you my far superior superiority."

"It's a junk heap."

"It made the Kessel Run in less than twelve parsecs."

She snorted. "And Rey called it garbage."

Shit. She had him there. "Still better than the Enterprise," he muttered, but he wasn't upset. Not in the least. It was fun to banter with her, especially over what nerdy stuff they enjoyed.

"Jean-Luc Picard," she declared. "That is the single thing I need to say to win this argument."

She had him there.

Except, "I preferred him in X-Men."

"Professor X," she said. "Yes, total BAMF."

He tilted his head to the side. "Is that some new-fangled Hollywood phrase?"

"Prof—" She shook herself. "Oh, you mean *BAMF?*"

"Yeah." He hadn't heard it, but then again, aside from the things he nerded out about, he didn't pay much attention to pop culture.

"No, it's what all the cool kids say nowadays," she told him. "BAMF stands for bad ass motherfucker." A grin. "As in Jean-Luc Picard."

"As in *my* Luke."

She scoffed. "God, no. He's too whiny for my tastes."

He set down his mug, straightened in his seat.

Soph immediately rose to attention. "What?"

"Them be fighting words." He rose, moved toward her.

"I—" She put her cup on the table, lifted her hands as though she were trying to placate him. "Now, no need to be hasty. *Star Wars* has plenty of good things going for it." She hopped to her feet when he got within arm's reach. "I even—*oh!*"

She squeaked when he scooped her up.

He ignored her protests and squirming. Instead, he tossed her over his shoulder and carried her into the house.

Rob wanted to head down the hall, to carry her into the bedroom and worship her like she deserved. But . . .

She deserved care and fun and teasing.

She deserved everything he'd had with Carmella—friendship and passion, laughter and kissing.

So, he veered left and carried her into the family room, plunking her onto the couch and tickling his fingers up under her ribs. "Take it back," he demanded, though he couldn't summon up any real force, not with how good it felt to be holding her so close.

She shrieked and batted at his hands. "Never! I will *never* take it back."

Then she proceeded to find a ticklish spot of his, just on the left side of his torso, one that had him squirming just as much as her.

Which made him forget any real thought of the *Star Wars* vs *Star Trek* Battle Royale. Instead, he relished the feel of her in his arms, the warm press of her body to his, the laughter filling the air, the joy in her pretty gray-blue eyes.

Eventually, though, they broke apart, breaths mingling, his hands in the hair that he couldn't stop playing with, hers on his shoulders, drawing him near.

"I'll never—" she was saying then seemed to recognize how close they were because her lips parted, her breathing sped, and her body drifted even closer. A heartbeat later, her mouth found his.

And perfection.

Heat, blistering heat mixed with the gentle prick of her fingernails. Soft moans breathed from her mouth to his as she kissed him until his lungs screamed. His cock felt harder than steel, his control completely frayed and one caress away from snapping, from surging up like a rogue wave and sucking them both under.

Only then did he set her away from him and stand.

His fingers trembled, his pulse pounded, but he forced himself to walk out to the deck, gather up the mugs, and bring them to the sink.

Then took a few seconds to rinse them and set them on the drying rack.

Control somewhat restored, he returned to the couch, the wonderful woman pushing mounds of brown hair out of her face, her eyes heavy-lidded, her mouth deliciously swollen from their kisses.

And he found he couldn't resist the temptation of her lips.

One more blistering kiss that obliterated that newfound control.

This time when he broke the embrace, cupping her cheek and studying those tempest blue-gray eyes for a heartbeat, Rob knew that control wasn't the only thing obliterated.

*He* was.

Shorn down and regrown.

Reborn for *this* woman.

"*Star Trek* is still better," she said, her breaths coming in rapid gusts, desire heavy in her gaze that was burning through him.

He laughed, even though his cock felt like it was going to break in half.

Because he knew, as he said goodbye, told her he'd see her the following day and forced his feet in the direction of the door, that he was the luckiest son of a bitch on the planet.

Because he'd found his soul mate.

Twice.

Now, he just had to convince Soph to let him keep her.

"SUNDAES?" he asked as they were packing up their knitting materials.

It was after class the next night, and he'd worked all day on a shitty job. Literally, *shitty* since he'd been repairing a cracked sewer pipe that had come in on an emergency call that morning, forcing him to delay his scheduled job for that day.

Which meant he was now going to be working Saturday.

Which also meant that he needed to get around to hiring an assistant contractor who could help him with just these types of situations.

Especially, if he was going to proceed with his Operation Soph plan.

At some point, she would need to go do Hollywood things— go shoot a movie or film some TV segment, but perhaps he could convince her to take a page out of Finn's book and make her home base here in Stoneybrook.

Here . . . with him.

For now, though, he just needed the woman to agree to sundaes.

She'd been jumpy from the moment she'd seen him in the parking lot. He'd been rushed, hair still damp from his shower, dumbass knitting bag glittering in his hand as he hurried to Misty's shop.

But there she'd been.

Walking with her head down as she moved toward the store.

And everything inside him had just . . . settled.

The crazed day had fallen away, the rushing, the irritation.

Because she was there.

Now, after most of the class, including Soph he was proud to say, had completed their second panel with the slightly more complicated stitch, she still wasn't looking at him, even though she'd accepted his help during the session with nary a complaint.

"Um," she murmured, eyes darting to something over his shoulder.

His heart sank, and he took her tote bag—seeing she must have repaired the strap—lifting it off her arm and setting it on the table, then drawing her to the side.

She brushed her fingers over a display of yellow yarn, nibbling at the corner of her mouth, still not looking at him.

His heart skipped, adding to the sinking.

Instead, it plummeted straight down to his toes, crawled under his boots, attempting to pummel itself for good measure. "Did I do something?" he asked, covering her hand where her thumb was rubbing back and forth across that yarn. "Did I hurt you?"

Her eyes finally found his. "Yes."

*Fuck.*

He staggered back a step.

She might as well have stabbed him in the heart, or he supposed he had done that himself. Because if he'd hurt her—

"You've made it impossible for me to think of anything except you," she whispered, taking his hand, drawing him closer when he would have retreated. "I have this ache inside me that only seems to be assuaged by you."

"Oh."

The response not remotely charming, not even in the *realm* of charming, but Rob was alternating between panic and relief, and he was too fucking out of practice with the female psyche.

"So, yes," she whispered. "Yes, I want to go to get sundaes with you."

"You do?"

She stepped close, ran her finger down his chest. "And yes,

afterward, I want to invite you back to my place." A smile. "Or go to yours."

"You do?"

Her smile growing. "Do you think the whole town will talk if I kiss you right now?"

His eyes flicked over her shoulder, saw that Misty and company were blatantly staring, not even trying to pretend they weren't watching the conversation taking place. "Yes," he told her.

Soph tilted her head from one side then to the other.

Then mischief slid over her face, and she shrugged.

"Fuck it," she whispered, throwing herself into his arms. Her body hit his with enough force to knock him back a step, but then her mouth landed on his, her breasts were flush to his chest, her legs around his waist.

And he was kissing her.

Or she was kissing him.

Or—

To take a page from her book, *fuck it*.

He gave the town something to talk about.

Then they went and got sundaes.

# SIXTEEN
## ICE CREAM NIRVANA

Soph

"AND EXTRA CHERRIES, PLEASE," she said to the cute teenage boy serving them at the diner a few blocks from *Tangled*.

She'd just ordered a Jumborama, per Rob's recommendation, and if she was going to down calories that she would have to work off tomorrow, then she figured she might as well go hog wild.

"You know," Rob said as the teenager with curly red hair and narrow, reed-like shoulders hustled off to put in their order, "I read somewhere that those cherries are the worst thing that a human can consume. Full of preservatives and colorings and pure sugar."

Her lips twitched. "Which is why you ordered extra cherries, as well?"

Laughing tiger's eyes. "Exactly." A beat. "If we're going to go down in flames, we might as well plummet together, am I right?"

"That sounds like the best thing I've heard in a long while."

And speaking of bests, the way he looked at her with warmth in his eyes, how he touched her, held her, laughed with her . . . yeah, there were a lot of bests in there.

He reached across the table, laced his fingers with hers. "What did you do today?"

"Beach. Nap. Read." A chuckle. "Would have been the perfect trifecta, if not for the script."

"What's wrong with it?"

She made a face. "I think this is the third rewrite, and I swear, the characters get less likeable with each version." Sighing, she leaned back in the booth, curling her legs up beneath her. "Worse is that I'm supposed to leave and film this in a month, but how the hell am I supposed to learn my lines if they keep changing everything?"

"I can help you," he offered.

And her heart went pitter-patter.

"You'd do that?"

"Shamelessly." He grinned . . . and more pitter-pattering.

"Why shamelessly?" she asked.

"Well—" The server set down two glasses of water, and Rob waited until he'd gone to finish answering. "Shamelessly because I think I would do pretty much anything to spend time with you."

"That's . . ." She trailed off, not sure what to say.

"Too much?" he asked, pulling his hand back.

"No." She reached for him, snagged it again. "Not too much." Her lips turned up, and she circled back to his previous statement. "Tell me, though, what would be beyond the *pretty much* for you?"

He tapped his chin. "Murder"—a shrug—"no, I suppose under the right circumstances, that would be on the table." His eyes met hers, the rage at the edges telling her exactly whom he might be willing to murder, given the chance.

Maybe that anger should have scared her, but instead, it warmed her.

She'd always worried that if someone found out the truth, they would look at her differently.

But Rob . . . he hadn't changed.

He knew it all and those swirling eyes, the gentle touch, the smiles and teasing—none of it had changed.

Heart squeezing, she traced the fingers of her free hand through the condensation on the outside of her water glass as she listened to him talk.

"Skinny dipping?" A shake of his head, a wicked grin. "No, I'd be happy to skinny dip with you."

She snorted. "I bet."

"Long walks on the beach, searching the mall for that one perfect handbag to go with your copious amounts of sexy-as-shit heels." He considered for a moment. "Also not beyond the *pretty much*. I'd happily do both of those."

Giggling now, she asked, "How about a farmer's market? Would you go to one of those with me? Walk up and down the aisles while I decide on the best variety of local honey?"

"Meh." He shrugged. "I'm an old hat at farmer's markets, and I can even tell you the difference between blackberry and acacia varieties of honey."

"Blackberry and . . . what?"

"Acacia." He waggled his brows. "Ooh, or maybe you'd prefer an alfalfa." A chef's kiss that had her busting a gut. "I bet you'd prefer a delicious alfalfa variety."

"That sounds disgusting."

He leaned back so the teenager could set down a pair of truly giant sundaes in front of them. "That it does," he said, handing her a spoon from a caddy near the end of the table before grabbing one for himself. "But it is surprisingly delicious, especially on toast with Lou's homemade bread."

"Who's Lou?"

"Baker in town." He gestured to her sundae. "Eat."

Her eyes narrowed. "I'm only eating because I want to, not because you went all caveman and ordered it."

He shrugged, dug in. "Whatever gets the ice cream into your sexy mouth sooner."

"Because you want to shut me up?"

A dark brow lifted, and he crossed around the table to sit next to her in the booth. "You think I'm dumb enough to bite on that question?" She started to huff but wasn't even mid-exhale before he snagged her spoon from her hand. "Yes," he said. "Apparently, I *am* dumb enough to answer that question." His lips dropped to her ear, voice silken, breath hot enough to make her shiver. "I want you to get this . . . *cream* in your mouth."

She inhaled, heat trickling between her thighs. "Didn't think you'd have dirty in you."

"Dirty *in* you?" That brow lifted again, and she actually blushed. Then he scooped up some ice cream and held the spoon up to her mouth.

Her lips parted before she could even process that she'd moved.

But then ice cream was on her tongue, the sweet treat melting on her taste buds and . . . *holy hell* but that was good. She stole the spoon back, scooped up a giant bite, before shoving it back in her mouth.

"Good, huh?" he asked, pointlessly, she supposed. "They make the ice cream from scratch in house."

She nodded, shoved him on the shoulder, and said, "Get on your side and eat this deliciousness before it melts and goes to waste." Of which, maybe half her words were decipherable, considering her mouth was plumb full of ice cream. But he got the message, sliding out of the booth and getting down to the business of devouring his own sundae.

"Oh!" he exclaimed after they were halfway through the "There is one thing I absolutely *will* not do."

Genuinely curious and enough ice cream consumed that she felt like she could pause in her hoovering for a moment, she asked, "What?"

Not exactly the most articulate of statements, but . . . ice cream.

She needed it, but she also wanted to know *every* single thing about this man.

"Musicals," he said in between much more reasonable bites than she was taking.

"Musicals?" she asked, spoon hovering two inches from her mouth.

He shuddered. "I can't do it. Carmella made me go see *Rent* once, and I stuffed my ears full of cotton during intermission."

"You didn't," she gasped.

"I did." He scooped up another bite. "And let me tell you that it was infinitely better that way."

"Well," she said. "Let me tell *you* that my favorite musical is *Rent*."

His lips curved. "So, I'm in for a world of hurt?"

"No." She reached across the table and bopped him on the nose. "You're in for a world of *good*."

He groaned.

But it turned out that she was right.

They were in for a world of good.

For a time.

# SEVENTEEN
## MORE UNLOCKED DOORS

Rob

FUCK, but he was exhausted.

It was Saturday evening, and he'd worked all day. But the job was done. The floor laid, the baseboards installed, and he had the next day off to spend with Soph.

Tonight, he needed to catch up on some sleep.

God, he hadn't pulled this many late nights since college.

Going back to Soph's after ice cream and staying up way too late talking about nothing . . . and making out. Because everything was better when he was able to hold and kiss and touch her.

Luckily, she seemed to like it when he did.

*And* liked to return the favor.

Which he certainly wasn't going to complain about.

But tonight she was busy with Finn and Shannon, and though he'd been invited, he was too fucking tired to summon up the energy to be social.

Pizza. A beer (one and no more than one considering his birthday adventures).

Then early to bed.

Currently, though, he was just summoning the energy to retrieve his cell from his pocket so he could plug it in.

"Later," he muttered, letting his head rest back on the couch.

The front door opened.

His nose started working right about the time he managed to summon the energy to peel his lids back and see who was invading.

Probably Misty wanting dirt on him and Soph. He'd already been interrogated from no less than a half dozen people in town about what was going on with him and the brunette beauty who'd utterly captivated him, but he wasn't one to kiss and talk, and he certainly wasn't going to give the gossip train in town any more fuel.

Nope, it was chugging along quite well without him.

His fault for bringing Soph to The Creamery.

Though, he would take the gossip any day of the week, especially after getting to witness her simple pleasure of eating that sundae.

Pleasure.

That was the most innocuous word for it.

Fuck. Truthfully, his cock still hadn't recovered.

Footsteps drew his attention to the front hall, to the opening where his intruder would appear in . . . three . . . two . . . one.

His heart stuttered. Squeezed. And he suddenly wasn't tired.

Because he was on his feet, moving toward Sophie.

"Hi," she murmured shyly.

He tucked a strand of her hair—unruly as ever—behind her ear. She kept blaming the sea breeze for the tangled strands, but Rob half-figured it was him and his inability to stop touching it.

Her hair was like his fidget spinner.

Only infinitely better.

"Hi," he said, bending around the pizza box and bag and pressing a light kiss to her mouth. "I thought you were busy tonight."

"Change of plans," she told him, nodding at her arms. "Turned out that I needed to see you."

Pleasure down his spine. His cock—well, the state of that particular body part was well-known and insistent on making its presence known as it pressed itself against the seam of his jeans.

He took the bag and box and carried both into the kitchen. "Well, I am really glad to see you, but I hope that you didn't mess up your plans for me."

"No." She came up behind him, wrapped her arms around his waist, hugging him tightly. "Turned out I was too tired to build late-night sandcastles with Rylie tonight. I wanted some junk food and . . ." He felt her shifting behind him as her sentence hung in the air for a few seconds. "*And* I brought *this!*"

A DVD appeared in front of his face.

"I didn't think people still used DVDs anymore," he said, once he'd stopped laughing about the appearance of an old school *Star Trek* disc.

"A desperate girl calls for desperate measures."

He spun, wrapped his arms around her waist. "I do have streaming, you know. We could have bought it."

She set the DVD on the counter, rested her head against his chest. "But it won't have the same quality as something from my personal collection." She tapped the cover. "This baby has been played on entertainment systems all over the world."

"Yeah?" he asked, running his hand up and down her arm. "Where?"

"Melbourne, Paris, Reykjavík, Tunisia." She tapped her chin. "Oh! It's even been to Antarctica."

His brows lifted. "*You've* been to Antarctica?"

Soph nodded. "I went as part of a documentary that was filmed last year. Fucking cold, but one of the best things I've ever done."

"Wow." A beat. "And you ruined it with *Star Trek*."

Swatting him lightly on the chest, she pushed out of his arms then plunked her hands on her hips, turning to survey the cabinets. "Where do you keep plates in this joint?"

He nodded at the one to the left of the sink. "There. Do you want a cup of tea?"

"Did I pound that sundae like it was my last meal on earth, even as I still am desperate to have another?"

"I'm taking that as a yes."

She laughed, moved to the cabinets and opened the door, retrieving two plates from inside. "Yes, it's a yes."

He put the kettle on, snagged two mugs. "I take it I've got to take you for another sundae sometime soon?"

"If you don't want a revolt on your hands, that's also a yes." Soph opened the lid on the pizza. "I wasn't sure what you liked, so I got two crowd-pleasers—pepperoni and Hawaiian."

He made a face.

Hers fell. "Oh shit. Are you a vegetarian? Or vegan? Or gluten-free? I—we can order something else—"

Rob crossed to her, kissed her cheek. "Pepperoni is great. The Hawaiian, I'll pass on."

"So you're not a vegetarian?"

He shook his head. "Or any of the other things. I'm just not a fan of pineapple on pizza." Shuddering, he turned back to the tea.

"No Hawaiian pizza. No musicals." Glancing back, he saw her nod, as though making a mental list.

"And what about you?" he asked. "What food don't you like?"

"Oysters. Raw ones, that is. I don't mind them fried, but

good grief, it seems like every single bigwig's party has to have an oyster bar." She gagged. "I can't stand that slimly feeling."

"Can't say I'm much of a fan of them myself," he agreed. "What else?"

"Hmm. Cow tongue," she said. "I tried that with friends once, and it's . . . well, it's not as horrible as I expected, but I don't think I want to eat it again, especially after I had nightmares of tongueless cows for weeks on end."

"That's a little too real for me," he said, filling the mugs with hot water when the kettle whistled and then putting in the tea bags so they could steep. "I prefer my food firmly processed."

Soph laughed. "Oh, how the Hollywood matrons would gasp and cling to their pearls with that statement."

"Feel free to use it next time you're at one of those oyster bar parties." He grabbed the mugs as she reached for the plates.

"I've already filed it away for future use."

Chuckling, he led the way into the family room, setting the mugs down and then taking the DVD from Soph. He loaded it in the player, snagged the remote, and handed it off to her. "Since you brought the torture."

She set it on the coffee table. "I'll torture you after pizza." A beat. "Tell me about your day? Any sewer pipes need emergency replacing?"

"No," he said, sitting next to her. "Thankfully, the job was just to patch some flooring that had gotten damaged. Although, once I pulled it up, I found mold, so the work became bigger than planned. I had to crawl under the house and replace a joist as well as some sub-floor."

"Why does it sound sexy when you say the word *joist?*"

He nearly choked on the bite of pizza. "Because . . ." He shook his head. "I have no idea."

Her laughter was warm and full of life, and he couldn't believe how much she'd opened up and relaxed since she'd first come to Stoneybrook. But it was as though her confession on that hillside, and the fact that he hadn't run screaming for said hills, had given her power . . . and taken it away from the memories that had swamped her.

Fuck, she was strong.

He couldn't imagine surviving what she had and somehow managing to become the lovely, kind person she was.

The world had turned its back on her at a pivotal moment in her life.

And she'd somehow put that behind her.

So strong and amazing and incredible and wonderful—even all those words together couldn't begin to describe the person Soph was.

"Earth to Rob," she said, nudging his thigh with her foot.

A quirk of hers he'd noticed—and something that felt so fucking great to be in the position to *do* that noticing—was that she was always curling her feet up underneath herself. Sometimes it was only one foot, like during the knitting class. Other times, like now or when they sat on her deck, she brought both up, pretzeling her legs in a way that had his knees screaming for mercy just looking at her.

"*Hello?*" she chirped, nudging him again.

"Sorry," he said, blinking rapidly, getting himself out of his head.

Her face closed down.

"What?"

She set her plate on the table, snagged his to do the same. Then she reached for his hands and stared deep into his eyes, making his stomach clench. *Shit.*

"Are you okay with me being here?"

He struggled for a moment to process what she was saying— or perhaps more accurately, *why* she was saying it. But before he could answer, she was on her feet, pacing the carpet in front of the coffee table.

"I'm sorry," she said, "I should have asked, should have made sure you were okay with it—"

"Tempest."

"This was the house you shared with your wife. *These*"—she waved a hand at the table—"were the things you probably did together." Her bottom lip trembled. "And I just barged in here uninvited and made myself at home like—like I belong or—"

He stood, rounded the table, and stood in the way of her pacing.

Then when she got close enough, he snagged her arms.

"This was your place with Carmella," she was babbling. "And it probably feels weird to have another woman on your couch when it used to belong to her, and it has to be—"

"Soph."

"—uncomfortable, especially since you didn't actually invite me," she said, ignoring him. "I should go." Her gaze darted toward the front door. "I should go and wait until sometime in the future when you invite me and—"

"*Sophie.*"

He kissed her.

Just wove his hand into those shining, luscious waves and let his mouth drop to hers—part to stop the flow of words, part to show her he knew exactly what woman was standing in his house, and part . . . well, perhaps part was to prove to himself that he didn't feel guilty for finally moving on.

No angst or remorse swelled within him, nothing dark gathered in his mind or heart. The only emotions that filled Rob were need—because fuck, did he want this woman—and the sense of utter rightness.

He'd felt it with Carmella in kindergarten.

And he'd felt it with Soph on the sidewalk out front.

No way was he going to continue living in the past when such a glorious present had somehow fallen into his lap—or had nearly run him over, as it was. And he certainly knew that he couldn't be too scared to live, too scared to grab on to this opportunity *and* find a way to keep Sophie forever.

He had to be in. All in.

Because he'd lost his other half once and understood how precious this was.

And . . . because Soph had lived through a past far darker than he and had found the courage to move forward.

So no, he wasn't going to continue in that half-life any longer.

"Carmella isn't here anymore," he said when they broke apart, brushing his thumb over her bottom lip.

"I'm sorry," she murmured, her eyes glistening with tears.

He cupped her cheek. "But you are, Tempest. You, who has survived so much more than anything I ever could, are."

"If I could bring her back for you, I would."

"No," he said, drawing her closer. "Maybe for a long time I would have wished that, would have given anything to go back. But"—he brushed his lips over hers—"then I met you. I've been lucky to spend time with you, and I know that even though I can't go back, can't change things, I can have something else."

She swallowed hard. "What?"

"I can have you," he said. "If you'll let me."

# EIGHTEEN
## MOVING BEYOND

Soph

"I . . . UM *WHAT?*" she sputtered.

Head spinning, she stepped away, pushed her hair off her face. He wanted her? Why?

*What the fuck?*

Not him. *Her.*

Because seriously, she'd spent so much time these last couple of weeks thinking about her past, making strides in not feeling shame for it, attempting to find the courage to grab on to something that wasn't empty. For the first time since the bad had overtaken her life, since her teenage fantasies had been shattered, Soph wanted something more. More than work. More than just going through the motions. She wanted a full life.

And she knew she deserved that life.

Finally, she had hope for the future. Hope for *a* future that wasn't what she'd always thought she'd deserved. Hope for a future that wasn't a punishment for her family's misdeeds and early fortunes.

She had hope for a future where she didn't have to worry about burdening someone with her baggage.

And now, someone wanted to give her that future.

But . . . she was chilled to the bone. Her breathing became ragged, her pulse hiccupping in her veins.

So close and she was fucking terrified to grab on to it.

A soft hand on her back had her startling, had the hand pulling away.

"No," she gasped, reaching behind her, clawing through the air until she felt Rob's arm, and then clinging to it like a lifeline, even as she bent forward at the waist, trying to catch her breath.

But it wouldn't be caught.

Each inhalation was short and staccato, jagged and painful, until her vision swam, and she felt like she was going to pass out.

She heard a curse, and then Rob's hand was gone.

That panic seized her tighter, but only for a moment. Because it only took a moment for Rob to scoop her up, to carry her back across the couch, and cradle her close.

"I-I'm sorry," she forced out, her throat still seizing. "I-I-I—"

He cupped her nape, ran a gentle thumb along the side of her neck. "Shh," he said. "It's okay, just watch me and breathe with me, okay?"

She nodded, her eyes locking with his.

"In, two, three," he said, inhaling. "Now, out, two, three." An exhale. "*That's* it, Tempest, slow and steady." Then he kept breathing, in and out, calm and easy, and she found that she was able to follow along.

And eventually, her pulse steadied, her muscles relaxed as the panic subsided.

"That's it," he kept whispering. "You're doing so good, honey. That's it."

Exhausted, she collapsed onto him, her arms wrapping around his waist, burying her face in his chest.

All the while, his hands remained tender, his voice kind.

"I'm sorry," she whispered to the wide breadth of muscle. "That was . . ."

His fingers tangled in her hair, tilted her face back. "Not unexpected."

She frowned.

"You hashed up a lot of past—and present—things in the last couple of weeks, you told *me* something you've been holding inside for a long time." He pressed a kiss to her forehead. "So, as I said, not unexpected."

Soph sighed and shook her head. "Why are you so wonderful?"

Half of his mouth ticked up. "I'll take the compliment." A kiss to her cheek. "Also, I'm a man who both knows what it's like to feel like the world is closing in around you, to be smothered with past memories, but also . . . I've emerged from the other side." He stroked a finger down her nose. "Because of you." A full smile now. "Because of you *and* your speeding through residential roads."

She growled. "*You* jumped out in front of *me.*"

His lips pressed to the base of her throat. "A fact I'm beyond grateful for."

"You—"

He kissed her, long and sweet and tender. Then long and hot and passionately. And when they broke apart, chests heaving, he said, "I'm also a man who's lost and lost big, which means I'm a man who knows he'd be a dumbass to not grab onto a fantastic, beautiful, smart, funny woman when she's right in front of him."

Heart pounding, hope singing in her veins, a lightness in her soul that she hadn't felt since she was thirteen had her saying back, "Especially, when she tries to run you over."

"Exactly," he said, laughing as he helped her sit up on the cushions next to him then plunked her plate of pizza in her lap.

His smile, his laughter was everything.

All those feelings inundating her, the hope for a future, the pleasure in just being with him.

Because she wanted this man, too.

And because she was going to let him in deep.

Oh shit.

Squee.

*Shit.*

*Squee.*

"One step at a time, Tempest." He picked up the remote from where it had gotten smooshed into the seam of two cushions and handed it to her. "I now give you permission to torture me with all your *Star Trek*-ness.

She grinned, that *squee* taking over, making her forget all about the *oh shit* feeling.

Then she hit play, began the so-called torture, and took a giant bite of pizza.

The perfect trifecta.

One made even more perfect when Rob slid his arm around her shoulders and cuddled her close.

# NINETEEN
## THE NIGHT BEFORE

Rob

BY ALL RIGHTS, he should be the one asleep.

And he *was* exhausted, but he couldn't bring himself to close his eyes, even though the DVD had long finished playing, long after Soph had relaxed against him, sleep tugging her under its tender embrace.

She'd lasted long enough for him to well appreciate her love of all things *Star Trek*, telling him fun facts, quoting dialogue, shushing him at the "important" parts.

But then her eyes had drooped, and she'd slumped against him.

And he'd gotten to just hold her.

And reflect.

And be forced to listen to the rest of the episodes.

*Star Wars* was still better.

Laughing to himself, Rob shifted on the couch, tugged Soph closer against his chest as he reclined back against the cushions, then closed his eyes against the glare of the TV.

Her sweet scent on his nose, he followed her into oblivion.

---

MOVEMENT WOKE HIM SOMETIME LATER, shifting along his torso, a whispered curse.

He tightened his arms when Soph went to slide off his chest. "Where do you think you're going?"

She startled, going stiff in his arms. "Jesus, you scared the crap out of me."

Running his hand up and down her back, he asked, "You need to go home?"

"I—" She nibbled at the corner of her mouth. "I should probably go and leave you to your rest."

"Do you *need* to go?"

Hesitation. Then, "No," she whispered.

"Do you *want* to go?"

Her tongue darted out, moistened her bottom lip. "No."

"Okay." He pushed to sitting in one abrupt movement, one arm swooping around her shoulders, the other under her knees. His back was aching, and he was too damned old to be sleeping on the couch. So, if she didn't *want* to go, didn't *need* to go, then he'd rather adjourn this to some place much more comfortable.

"Rob?" she asked as he strode up the stairs.

He paused. "Too much?"

A shake of her head. "I just . . . I'm not—that is, I don't think I'm ready."

His heart squeezed, another piece chipping off, offering itself up on a silver platter to this woman. "Just to sleep."

Wide eyes on his.

"Okay?"

"Okay," she whispered.

He kept walking, carrying her into the bedroom and placing her on her feet, then moving over to his dresser and pulling out a T-shirt. "In case you want to be comfortable." A kiss to the top of her head. "I'll go lock up."

She nodded and he moved to do that, but her words stopped him when he was almost in the hall. "I thought you didn't lock doors in this town."

"True," he said. "But I definitely lock up when I have a beautiful woman in my bed."

Blushing, she ducked her head.

"Soph?" he asked, worried for a moment that she was uncomfortable.

"Go on then," she said. "And hurry back. I like it when you hold me."

Cock twitching at the sight of that sweet smile, he headed downstairs, gathering up the plates and mugs, placing them in the sink, then shoving the pizza into a container and putting it in the fridge.

He peeked in the bag she'd brought, just to make sure it wasn't something that would spoil, and smiled when he saw the bagels inside. She might not be ready for anything more intimate than kisses, but she'd definitely had sleeping over somewhere in her mind, bringing over both dinner *and* breakfast. And she was letting him hold her.

So yeah, his plan to keep her was gaining steam.

He turned off the TV, locked the front door, and headed upstairs, his heart stuttering when he crossed the threshold.

Soph was coming out of the bathroom, her hair long and gleaming, her feet bare. Well, more than her feet. His shirt only covered her to the tops of her thighs, so there was a lot of glorious bare skin on display.

"You okay?" she whispered.

He nodded, crossing over to her and taking her hand. "Let's

sleep," he said, coaxing her over to the bed and peeling back the covers.

She crawled in, he covered her up, then went back to his side.

It should be awkward, him crawling into bed with a woman who wasn't his wife. The blankets and sheets had changed—he'd bought new ones the day he'd packed up Carmella's belongings—but he hadn't ever had another woman besides her in this bed.

So, it should have been awkward.

But it wasn't.

Just as everything else with this woman . . . it felt normal. Comfortable. Not the least bit strange or uncomfortable.

This was right.

She rolled over onto her side, facing him, her expression just visible between the moon's rays drifting through the curtains and the soft glow of the nightlight in the corner. "Hi," she whispered.

He chuckled. "Hi."

"I'm not tired."

His lips twitched, and he twined a strand of her hair around his finger. "Well, you just did wake up from a nap." A beat. "Should I go get your world-traveled DVD?"

Soph giggled. "No," she said. "I'd rather—" Her words were cut off by a yawn.

He ran the back of his fingers over her jaw. "You sound tired to me."

"Maybe." She inched closer, tracing circles on his chest.

"You should sleep."

"I'd rather just talk to you," she said, closing the distance between them and resting her head on his shoulder.

Love—*love*—for this woman bloomed in his heart, and he wanted to stay up for hours, talking to her, finding out every like and dislike, learning everything that made her tick. But they were both tired and needed their rest. "I can expound on the gloriousness of different varieties of nails if you need help falling asleep."

Another giggle, her snuggling closer. "No, thanks," she murmured. "I want to hear more about you."

"More about the boring small-town carpenter?" He laughed. "That'll definitely put you out."

A light swat on his shoulder. "Stop."

"What do you want to know?"

"Do you like to travel?"

He nodded. "Love it."

"What's your favorite place to visit?"

"I really enjoyed New Zealand," he said. "Carmella and I honeymooned there. And Japan was pretty epic, though I was not a fan of the humidity."

"Don't you get that here?" she asked.

"Inland, yes. But on the coast and with the sea breeze, we're spared the worst of it." He rested his chin on the top of her head. "What about you? Do you like to travel?"

"When it's for me, yes," she said. "When it's for work, it depends."

"Why depends?"

Her lips pressed to the base of his throat. "Depends on where I'm going. Sometimes it's really cool, and the schedule means I can visit places I've always wanted to see. Other times, I feel like I'm in these awesome locations and I see nothing more than my hotel room and the shooting locations." One shoulder lifted and dropped, her head tilting back so he could see the amusement in her eyes. "Oh, the humanity. Poor little rich girl complaining about having to travel the world."

He snorted. "So tough." He brushed his lips across hers.

"But seriously, there are always going to be things about your job that you don't like. Even if it's a fancy one like yours."

"What's yours?"

"My fancy job?" he asked.

"No, what don't you like about yours?"

"Besides sewer lines that need replacing?"

She smirked before dropping a kiss to his jaw. "Besides sewer lines."

"Ah." He tapped his finger to his chin. "I actually really like my job. It's decidedly not fancy, but I like to fix things, to make them look nice for my clients."

"Those all seem like good things." She poked him lightly. "I want to hear the bad."

"Well, the plumbing, sewer-related or not, is definitely not my favorite part—though I have a sub who takes care of most of that, thankfully," he said. "But if I was going to pick the most tedious, odious, and whatever other -ious adjectives that fit with those other two, I would say trim."

"Like cutting things?"

His lips twitched. "No. Well, *yes*. But it's the baseboard and crown molding, the tiny fiddly pieces that go around windows and doors." He shuddered. "God, that's the worst, and always at the end of the job when I just want to be done and moving onto the next shiny thing. Which is probably bad. I should enjoy the process. But there *is* something exciting about looking ahead."

"I feel you," she said. "Why do you think actors are constantly jumping around into new roles? We're the ultimate" —a yawn—"*look squirrel!* crew."

"Hmm." He held her close again, running his hand up and down her back.

"You're trying to coax me into sleep with all that hand-rubbing, aren't you?"

It was his turn to yawn. "I'll neither confirm nor deny."

"Well, confirm or deny all you want," she said, wrapping her arm around his waist. "It's working."

"Sleep now," he whispered, letting his own eyes slide closed.

"Oh"—another yawn—"'kay."

Then there were no more words, just slowing breaths, sleep creeping closer, and complete and utter rightness in his arms.

# TWENTY
# THE MORNING AFTER

Soph

SLOWLY COMING AWAKE, she yawned and stretched.

Or attempted to anyway.

Because a heavy arm and leg were draped over her, tucking her against a hard, hot *male* body. Pinning her to Rob.

Yes. To Rob.

She knew who it was before she opened her eyes. She knew who it was by the scent in her nose, by the way he held her—snug and close, but still with care. Even when the man was unconscious, he still held her gently.

Soph didn't want to move, didn't want to slide out of that warm, cozy place.

But her bladder was calling.

Loudly.

So, she began the process of wiggling out of his embrace. First nudging his leg off hers—or attempting to, anyway. Because the moment she shoved it off her thighs, he slid it right back over her, tucking her more firmly beneath him, his arms drawing tighter.

Sighing, she started again, this time with his arms.

But between both of his, the blanket and his leg wrapped around her, she might as well be fighting an octopus.

And truthfully, she wasn't struggling all that much, especially when it felt so nice to have him wrapped so tightly. In fact, if she didn't have to use the restroom, she probably would have been shifting closer, rubbing against him like a cat demanding scratches.

It was just . . . she had to pee.

"Rob," she said softly when his hand slid down her spine and cupped her cheek—and not the one on her face. He squeezed the globe of her ass, angled her hips against his, and all but took her breath away when he ground the hard length of his erection against her.

*God*, that was good.

Really good.

In fact, it was almost enough to make her forget she had to pee.

He rolled and she was suddenly beneath him, those tiger's eyes hot as they bored into hers, still laced with sleep, his hair deliciously rumpled.

"Morning," he said, voice husky, like roughed-up velvet skating over her skin.

"Morning," she whispered, her hands coming up to rest on his shoulders, kneading lightly into the hard planes of his muscles.

His head dropped, lips finding her jaw, her throat. "Morning," he said again, hot breath coating her skin and making her shiver,

"Morning," she whispered again, her hands coming up to his hair, tugging lightly.

A nip to her neck, just where it met her shoulder. "I won't say morning again," he murmured, teeth tugging her

T-shirt slightly to the side, tongue dipping beneath the fabric.

"Mmm," she said, arching up against him.

He groaned, hips dropping to hers.

"Oh fuck," she whispered, her trip to the bathroom completely forgotten under the intensity of that gaze, the feel of his body against hers, that silken tongue darting against her skin.

She jerked when his palm slipped under the fabric of the shirt, traced against her stomach.

"No?" he asked.

She shook her head. "No, I mean *yes*," she added when he started pulling his hand out, snagging his wrist to halt the retreat. "No, don't stop," she ordered.

The ghost of a smile.

His palm slid back, tracing lazy circles on her abdomen. "Can I kiss you?" he asked. "Or should we pause for tooth-brushing and ablutions?"

"Ablu—*ah*—tions?" she asked, sighing when his fingers made it to the bottom of her breast. Back and forth. Back and forth. Back and— "Who uses that word nowadays?"

"I do."

But she barely heard his response.

Because his thumb had skimmed over her nipple.

"Oh!" she gasped, pleasure shooting through her.

"Too much?"

She thanked God that this question of his was easier to answer. "No," she said, her fingers clenching in his hair.

"And kissing?" he asked, mouth temptingly close, that thumb still sending sparks of desire through her to coil heavy in her abdomen, to snake down between her thighs. "Yes or no?"

Luckily, this one didn't require a verbal answer. She simply tugged his head down and kissed him.

It should have been gross—with their respective morning

dragon breaths—but it wasn't. Nothing about anything with this man was gross. The kiss was scorching and perfect and filled her with so much need that her hands were shaking, her thighs trembling as they clenched against him, as he let more of his weight fall against her, as she ground herself against his cock.

And all the while his thumb continued with the light brushes, those back and forths, driving her absolutely mad as he teased one nipple and then the other.

As though he had all the time in the world to keep coaxing her up the edge with those soft touches, as though he weren't hard and insistent against her, as though he wasn't driving her insane.

"Still okay?" he murmured when he broke the kiss.

She nodded, head thrown back on the pillow, hips jerking.

He rolled her nipple between thumb and forefinger and she cried out, his name on her lips. Those fingers continued working as he kissed his way down her throat, as he leaned back enough to slowly lift her shirt, pausing to make sure she was with him. And while the gesture was sweet and considerate, it also pricked her temper.

"I won't break, dammit," she said, yanking the fabric up and attempting to get it over her head, fighting with the damned piece of cotton until he helped her get it off, exposing herself to his gaze.

He was frozen for long moments, eyes scorching into hers then dropping down, his stare almost tangible as it alighted on her breasts. "You said you weren't ready, Tempest."

She glared, knowing she was unreasonably annoyed because she *had* said that. "Well, I'm ready now."

His lips twitched. "Really?"

"Really." She crossed her arms, watched him study her almost naked form and swallow again.

"Well . . ."

Her brows pulled together. "Well, what?"

Tiger's eyes managing to make their way back up to hers, and she was surprised to see that the edge of reserve in them.

Heart sinking, she clenched her abdomen.

Was *he* not okay with this? Was it too soon?

"Rob?" she asked gently. "What is it?"

"I—" His cheeks went a little pink.

Now her heart *squeezed*, along with her gut twisting itself into knots. "We don't have to do this," she said, reaching for her shirt. "We can wait until you're ready."

He chuckled, and it rasped down her skin. "Oh, *I'm* ready. It's just . . ."

Oh, shit, what if it was her? What if he didn't like something about *her*?

"I've only done this with one other person," he said, cheeks still slightly tinged with red, but his eyes on hers. "I might not be able to . . ." His gaze darted away then back to hers. "Promise me that you'll tell me if I do anything you don't like."

That knot in her stomach unlaced.

Her heart, however, it kept squeezing.

Because this man . . . fuck, he was doing a hell of a job of stealing it.

"I promise," she said, wrapping her arms around his shoulders and lying back on the mattress, taking him with her. He didn't hesitate, just brought all of that glorious muscled heat back on top of her. But other than moving with her, he didn't resume his earlier ministrations, not until she said again, "I promise."

Then he *moved*.

His mouth dropped to hers, tongue dipping inside, tempting her into a kiss that sent her pulse thundering and her pussy clenching. His hands returned to her breasts, cupping and molding them in those calloused palms, making her moan. He drank it down, answered with one of his own before tearing his lips from hers and dragging them along her throat, nipping across her collarbones.

And then . . . glories of all gloriousness, he sucked her nipple deep into his mouth.

She screamed, dug her nails into his shoulders.

His stiffened.

"Sorry," she said, breaths coming in short puffs, immediately releasing him.

"Don't," he told her, covering one of her hands with his, a wolfish smile on his mouth. "I like it."

She nodded, smiling back.

But the smile didn't last long, not when the dangerous man returned his attention to her breasts, not when he went back to sucking her nipples deeply, using his tongue and teeth to send her desire skyrocketing. He lavished attention to her breasts for long minutes, only leaving after turning her into a ball of need, every nerve on fire, aching, *needing* this man.

Then he began kissing his way down her torso, dragging his mouth across her rib cage, nipping at her hip bone on one side then the other, laving her belly button with his tongue.

Then laving something else.

Because he slid down, spread her thighs, and licked her pussy in one long, wet, *hot* stroke.

Gasping, her fingers went tight on his shoulders again, her hips bucked, and she ground herself against his mouth when he found . . . just . . . the . . . right . . . spot. "Oh, God!"

"Mmm." He nuzzled closer, redoubled his efforts, tongue and thumb working in tandem, his hot eyes coming up to meet hers and holding hers captive. Stomach clenching in the best way from his intense stare, she tugged him closer, held him even more tautly. He paused in his attentions, a sexy smile on lips glistening with her damp heat, but it was the passion in his gaze that had her nerves tingling, that made her nipples tighten into beads and ache for his mouth. Then he did something with that thumb, with that tongue that had her head falling back, her eyes open and unseeing on the ceiling.

"Yes?" he murmured against her.

"Oh!" She bucked against him as her pleasure wound tighter. "Fuck."

"Yes?" he asked again, increasing the pressure and speed with his fingers, sending pleasure scorching through her. But she wanted his mouth on her again. She wanted him doing that thing with his tongue on her clit. "Tempest?" He waited until she looked at him. "Yes?"

Her temper frayed, head jerking up to glare at him. "What part of my moans have confused you?" She gestured between her legs. "Get back to it already."

He grinned. "Get back to"—a flick of his tongue—"this?"

She groaned. "Stop teasing."

"Why?" A stroke of his thumb. "I like teasing you."

"Because—ah—I—"

"Only slightly less than I like seeing you lose that temper of yours."

She gasped—outraged—but that outrage quickly turned into pleasure when he dropped his mouth back down and, slow and steady, built her need to a cresting point as he circled her clit with his tongue, slid a finger inside, and—

*"Oh, God!"*

She exploded.

That was the only way she could describe it. One second, she was herself, the next she was in pieces, scattered to the wind.

But never fear, Rob gathered them all up, cradled them carefully, and pieced her back together.

Then crawled up her body to cradle *her* closely.

Warm arms wrapping around her, a strong body pressed to hers, gentle hands tracing patterns on her back . . . and an insistent cock pulsing against her abdomen. Pulsing, but its owner just holding her, calmly and steadily and not making any move to come atop her, to slide inside, to—

Desire anew.

Embers flaring, licking at the inside of her skin. She brought her hand to his chest, glided it down until her fingertips brushed the hard length of him.

He groaned, thrust against her, but just as she gripped his cock, reveling in the feel of his velvet-covered steel, he brushed her hand away, capturing it and bringing it up to his mouth. "Not today, Tempest," he murmured, kissing her palm.

Her heart, fuck, but she could swear it had never actually beat until she'd met this man.

And now, it absolutely pounded for him.

Arching up, she pressed her mouth to his, wrapped her leg over his thigh, and pushed him onto his back.

He broke away. "Soph."

She silenced him with a kiss. "I'm ready, if you are." She ran her fingers over his jaw, his stubble bristling against the tips and making her shiver.

"Sweetheart," he began, eyes sliding closed when she began to kiss her way down his chest. "I want you, but just last night—"

"I like you," she blurted, and his lids flew open, gaze locking with hers. *Like* was a mere shadow of a description for what was in her heart, but it was too soon, too fast for her to examine what was beneath that too closely. For now, she just wanted . . . "I like you and I want you and I just want to stop living in my head or through my characters." She pressed a kiss to the spot over his heart, felt it beating as rapidly as her own. "I want this . . . if you're there with me."

His hands were resting on her hips, and they clenched when she said the last.

Then she found herself on her back, him poised above her. "You're sure?" he asked.

"I think I said that already," she replied tartly.

His grin was sexy as hell, making her clench in need, in *remorse* that she was beneath him but still wasn't *full* of him.

"I guess I'd better get my ass in gear."

She laughed, he reached into the nightstand and extracted a condom before shoving off the boxer briefs he wore.

And suddenly, he was naked.

Lucky her.

# TWENTY-ONE
## SURVIVING THE STORM

Rob

HE WAS POISED OVER HER, harder than he'd ever been in his life and shaking, absolutely feeling like this was his first time all over again.

Soph slipped the condom from his trembling fingers and rolled it down his cock, and Rob wouldn't be lying if he said that even that slight touch had him threatening to explode.

Just the sight of her beneath him—cheeks pinkened with desire, her flush spreading out along her chest, her breasts with their hardened nipples begging for his mouth. He was desperate to touch her everywhere, to lick and stroke every inch of her skin, but he was just as desperate to plunge inside, to thrust and thrust and pound her over the edge.

He'd never been this close to losing control.

He'd always approached lovemaking with determination and finesse, making sure Carmella was pleased before he tumbled over the edge.

But he'd never been this close to losing *himself*.

For the first time since his life had taken that sharp left turn a few weeks ago, he was terrified—of what he would gain, of what he might lose, of—

A gentle touch on his cheek, hands drawing his head down to hers until their breaths mingled and her lips found his ear. "It's okay," she murmured. "This is just about us, about what we feel. Not the past or present or future. Just *us*."

The air left his lungs in a rapid exhale and he pulled back slightly, cupped her jaw, and nodded. "Just us."

Then she brought her lips to his, tongue dipping into his mouth, hands coming to his shoulders, nails pricking his skin.

And he stopped worrying, stopped thinking.

He just . . . felt.

Soph's curves beneath him, her mouth on his, her hands pulling him closer. He dragged his lips away from hers, nipped his way down her throat, sucked deeply on one nipple and then the other. His hand dipped between her thighs, using the rhythm and pressure he'd discovered she liked best to rouse her desire, to bring her as close to the edge as he felt—until her hips were jerking against his touch, her breaths coming in short gasps, moans tumbling out of her mouth one after another.

Her eyes locked with his as she ordered, "*Now.*"

He didn't have any strength to resist this woman.

Instead, he guided her leg around his hip, positioned himself, and . . . then thrust home.

His forehead dropped to hers on a groan, the heat of her, the way she clenched so tightly around him, bringing him within mere millimeters of the edge, but he forced himself to not thrust again and again and again. He forced himself to pause and ask, "Okay?"

Lids flying open, pale gray-blue eyes the most accurate depiction of a tempest he'd ever seen, especially when they flashed—equal parts amusement and annoyance. But then her expression softened, the tempest cleared, and she arched her neck, tilting her head so her lips rested against his, their breaths mingling, and her next words were spoken directly into his mouth. "Better than okay, baby. Now, move."

He moved.

Sliding out, pressing deep, trying different angles until her breath hitched, until her eyes closed, and her head pressed back into the pillows. Then he kept at that angle, continued the speed and pressure and her other thigh wrapped around his waist, heels digging into his ass, hips meeting him stroke for stroke.

It was incredible.

It was perfect.

It was . . . erasing any semblance of thought.

Rob could only process how good she felt, tight and hot. He could only hear the blood pounding in his ears, her moans. He could only—

"Fuck," he hissed when she tightened around him, his orgasm coiling at the base of his spine. "Please, say you're there."

"I—" Her head thrashed. "Don't stop. Don't—"

She broke off on a moan, hips jerking against his, her cheeks bright pink, lips parted, and . . . then she was over the edge, clenching around him, drawing him alongside her to plummet over that cliff as wave after wave of pleasure poured over him.

Drowning in that tempest.

Winds and waves, sea and storm yanking him beneath the surface of the water . . . and then the tempest cleared.

Then he was opening his eyes and staring into those of a brilliant blue-gray.

And he felt like a ship that had somehow survived a deadly gale, sails slightly battered, mast cracked as it glided its way into port.

And finally arriving home, comfortable in the knowledge that all could be repaired.

ABOUT TWO MINUTES after the most intense and fulfilling sexual experience of his life, Soph stiffened in his arms.

Then jumped out of bed.

"Soph?" He reached for her, missed.

"I—" A shake of her head before she ran for the bathroom.

That pleasant feeling faded, and he hurried to his feet, grabbing his underwear and stepping into them before moving to follow Sophie into the bathroom. Then he paused, realized he couldn't just barge in like he might have with Carmella. He should knock.

So, he did.

The water came on in the sink.

"Just a second," she called.

But it was more than a few seconds, and after a minute, Rob simply ran out of patience. He turned the knob and strode in. "It's okay if you're—"

He didn't finish the sentence.

Because he turned around, his cheeks feeling hot.

Soph was on the toilet. Soph was *using* the toilet.

He stepped out, closed the door behind him. A minute later, he heard the toilet flush, her footsteps moving to the sink, the stream of water changing as she washed her hands, and then she came out of the bathroom, wrapped in a towel and fucking beautiful in the early morning light.

Except . . . he'd barged in on her.

His eyes met hers then darted away.

"Sorry," he said. "I thought—"

"It was an emergency."

Lips parting, he glanced back at her.

She giggled. "Well, it was an emergency *before* our horizontal shenanigans. After, it was . . . I don't know, whatever is worse than an emergency."

He snorted.

She smacked him lightly. "It's your fault, I'll have you know. I was trying to wiggle away from you before you got all . . . *manly* and sexy and distracted me with two freaking orgasms."

"It was your fault," he said, taking her hand, leading her back to bed. He had plans for her, and they involved her captive on that mattress.

But he needed to make his own trip to the bathroom to clean up.

Maybe he could coax her back into bed, tempt her to remain naked permanently with treats and copious amounts of tea.

Hmm.

Now, that thought presented some serious consideration. She'd be sprawled out there and ready for his lips and fingers and tongue. First, he'd spend long minutes on her breasts. Then trace the smattering of freckles on her torso with his tongue. *Then* he'd taste her again.

And only after that would he slide home, riding her until he found the pattern and rhythm that made her lose any semblance of control.

"What are you thinking?" she asked, drifting closer.

"Hold that thought," he said, nudging her onto the mattress before disappearing into the bathroom, quickly taking care of the condom and other necessities, then came back out, hoping he'd been quick enough to find her still in bed.

She was.

Lucky him.

He swapped the dirty underwear for clean then crawled back into bed, taking Soph into his arms. "Are you done holding that thought?" he asked lightly.

"Depends," she said, cuddling up to him. "Are you going to tell me what you were thinking?"

"That you are fucking gorgeous and that I want to lick chocolate syrup off every inch of you."

"That sounds both kinky and sticky," she said, giggling.

"I was also wondering," he said, parting the sides of her towel and tugging her closer. "Why you were wearing this?"

She stilled.

He tensed, wondering if he'd overstepped. "Shit," he muttered. "I didn't mean to bring up something that would make you uncomfortable." He reached for the towel, started to wrap it around her.

But then her chin came up, and determination filled her expression.

His heart squeezed. "It's the scars."

She made a face. "Yes," she said. "I know you already saw them, but that was different. It wasn't a full view of my entire back, and it wasn't under fluorescent lighting, and I like to pretend that I'm tough and unaffected by them, that I'm not ashamed but . . ."

"You're insecure about them."

She bit her lip and hesitated. Rob experienced another bolt of rage that this woman, this incredible woman had endured what she had. But he couldn't take this away from her, and he truly didn't care about the scars. He'd felt them on her back when he'd touched her, had seen them in the sunlight, so no, he didn't give a shit what they looked or felt like. What he hated was that she'd been hurt, that her skin bore a memory of the things she'd overcome. It wasn't fair she had to shoulder that atop everything else she'd survived.

But he didn't give two fucks about the actual scars.

"I shouldn't be," she whispered. "But they're bad enough that I have it written into my contract for a body double any time my back needs to be on film. Bad enough that my wardrobe always covers it—even in the skimpiest swimsuit scene, I make sure to have a cover-up. And I don't ever take it off—no matter what the director wants."

"Tempest, I truly don't care about your scars."

Her face softened. "I . . . well, I can't say that I *know*, since I don't make a habit of showing them to anyone," she said. "But I think if there was ever a person who truly didn't care about them, I think it would be you."

"Do you want me to get you a shirt you can wear?"

Mouth curving, she rested her palm on his chest. "I really like you. You know that?"

He kissed the top of her nose. "Well, I really, *really* like you."

That mouth tipped up further. "Is this where I say, *really* times three?"

Laughing, he pressed a kiss to her lips, tasting her smile on his tongue, knowing he was so lucky to be here with this woman. "If you want," he told her when they broke apart for air. "But then I'd have to one-up you by saying times four."

"Competitive, are we?"

"You should see me during Phase Ten."

Brows drawing together, she asked, "What's that?"

"You don't know?" he asked with mock-outrage. "How can Hollywood's favorite leading woman not know what Phase Ten is?"

She punched him lightly on the shoulder. "Are you going to tell me?" she grumbled. "Or just keep gloating?"

"Oh, no, I'm not going to tell you. I'm going to *show* you."

"Hmm."

He rolled onto his back, tugged her on top of him.

Wickedness in her eyes, her smile, her hands as they slipped down his chest. "Or maybe I'm going to show *you?*"

# TWENTY-TWO

## CARD SHARK

Soph

SUNSHINE WAS POURING in through the windows, dappling Rob's skin with streaks of gold, bringing out the red undertones in his hair.

He had no right to be so pretty.

He had no right to devastate her heart so completely.

Sighing, but desperate now to brush her teeth and shower, she forced herself to push off his chest, his pulse still thudding beneath her palms, and sat up.

"Okay?" he asked, starting to sit up.

"Shower," she said. "And toothbrushing."

He groaned, flopped back. "Are you always this energetic in the morning?" he groused.

"When a man gives me almost a half-dozen orgasms"—fucking hell that was a record—"then yes."

"Four isn't a half-dozen," he grumbled, tucking the blankets around them and holding her captive against his chest again. All things considered, she didn't mind being his prisoner, not if it meant being surrounded by him and his yummy scent, and not if he kept holding her close.

And playing with her hair.

Because *God*, she really liked it when he played with her hair.

But she had a reputation to maintain. She wasn't going to be reduced to a limp noodle just because she'd found an awesome man . . . who could give her awesome orgasms.

"Fine," she said, shifting so she could rest her chin on her folded hands. "A third of a dozen. Better now?"

A grunt was her only response, and when she glanced up at his face, she saw he'd closed his eyes, though his lips were turned up at the edges. "Yes," he said. "I'll take a third of a dozen."

Laughing, she twisted and tugged lightly at the blankets, trying to free herself. After a moment of making absolutely no progress except to get drawn somehow even closer, she sighed and plunked back down on top of him. "I see this is going to be a problem."

"Shh," he said. "*Sleep.*"

"I'm not tired."

"I am," he muttered. "Some wench kept me up late last night and then exhausted me this morning."

"I think this morning was your fault."

"Nope. Uh-uh," he said. "I was trying to be the responsible one."

She snorted but couldn't deny that she had been the driving force behind their mattress antics—or at least maybe slightly more than halfway responsible. He had given her all those orgasms after all. "Meh," she said. "Responsibility is overrated."

He didn't respond, just kept his eyes closed.

"You know what *isn't* overrated?"

A grunt.

"Getting out of bed in the morning when the sun is shining so brightly!" she sing-songed.

He slit open his lids. "I'm not giving you third of a dozen orgasms anymore."

She laughed, bouncing lightly on his chest. "Liar."

A shrug. "Yup."

"Let's get up and play."

Amusement danced its way across his face. "Play what?"

She threw up an arm. "Anything!"

He put a pillow over his head. "Nope."

Grinning and having more fun with this man than she had with anyone in a long time, she just yanked it free and went back to bouncing on his chest. "Rise and shine, baby," she said, ignoring his grunt of displeasure. "If you get up right now, I'll let you play with me in the shower.

Magically, he summoned the energy to get out of bed.

Also, magically, he summoned the energy to make her third of a dozen orgasms turn into a half-dozen.

---

"Read 'em and weep," she said cheerfully, putting down her final combination of cards (one set of five of a kind and one set of three of a kind).

Rob sighed in disgust.

Probably because she'd been very far behind for the first half of the game.

Then she'd crushed him resoundingly.

"You're a card shark," he mock-grumbled, laying down his cards and scooping her onto his lap. He'd convinced her to play on the couch, mostly because he'd promised to let her pick what was on TV in the background and had made them a giant bowl of popcorn to share.

Not that she was hungry.

He'd taken the bagels she'd brought and turned them from breakfast to lunch—since, by the time they'd made it out of the bathroom, it was much closer to noon than not. And though the bagel sandwiches were loaded with lunchmeat and cheese along with *all* the condiments, nothing had been as good as that morning in the bedroom *and* bathroom.

Bedroom because . . . obviously.

Bathroom because . . . God, the man never failed to make her heart melt. He'd warmed up the shower then tucked her under the hot water before retrieving extra towels—one for her body and one for her hair, smart man that he was—and had even produced some color-saving shampoo and conditioner from somewhere.

Well, not somewhere, since certainly it had belonged to Carmella.

He'd presented it with an apology in his eyes, as though she could ever harbor any ill-will toward the woman. Not only was she gone, but she'd also loved this wonderful man in a way that had stayed with him for years.

Obviously, Soph didn't like the idea of him hurting, least of all for years, but she *did* like the idea of him having cherished moments and happy times with his late wife.

So, she'd just thanked him for the shampoo and conditioner and had used it, sending up a mental prayer that Carmella was content and joyful, wherever she had ended up.

Later, when he'd finally gotten into the shower, coming close to share the stream, her stomach had tightened in anticipation. She knew he'd be able to see the scars fully, without her bra or T-shirt blocking parts of them, and under the bright lights of the bathroom. Part of her had still worried he be disgusted by them, that she had been wrong about him and he'd look at her differently because of them.

But he hadn't looked at her differently.

He'd just stroked his hand up and down her spine, just kissed her lightly on her mouth, and then bent to repeat the gesture on each of the heavy, ridged marks.

Then he'd washed her body with a spicy-scented soap that told her where at least part of his yummy scent came from.

Now the sun was setting, and she knew that she'd need to go back to her place soon. One, because she was out of clean clothes. Two, because he would need to go to work in the morning and she wouldn't do anything to jeopardize his business.

But she didn't want to.

She wanted to fall asleep in his arms and wake him up with her wiggling again. She wanted to spend every second with this man, especially since her time in this town was going to be coming to an end in just a few weeks.

God, that made her sadder than it should. But she'd committed to the film and others. She wouldn't be able to look at herself in the mirror if she didn't honor her commitments—or got in the way of Rob honoring his. Which meant she should go, even though she wanted to soak up every minute.

"I should—"

He nuzzled her throat, lips pressing to a spot just beneath her ear that never failed to make her shiver.

"Stay tonight?" he asked, fingers coming up to tangle in her hair. "I'm not quite ready to let you go."

"I don't want to mess up what you have to do."

"Why would you mess me up?"

She leaned back in his lap, ran her fingers through his hair. "You have to work tomorrow."

A smile. "Not sure what that has to do with tonight."

"I—" She sighed. "Well, I'm leaving in two weeks. It might be better if we didn't get too used to each other."

"Fuck that."

Soph blinked.

"If you have to leave in two weeks, then I want to have every possible moment with you." A beat. "And after you go," he murmured, "I want those moments, too."

"But—"

He brushed a kiss to her jaw. "But what?"

"What if things change when I go?"

His arms tightened around her. "Things *will* change," he said, far more confidently than she felt, "but the important stuff won't."

"How do you know?"

A warm hand placed over her heart, and she wondered if he felt how fast it was thudding in her chest.

Probably.

But she couldn't bring herself to care when he brought his lips to her ear and whispered, hot breath making her shiver. "I *know*."

Then his mouth dropped onto hers.

And she forgot all about the reasons she shouldn't stay.

Instead, she slept peacefully in Rob's arms that night.

But better yet was waking up with those arms still around her.

# TWENTY-THREE
## ALL THE GRUMPS

Rob

"HOW DARE YOU?" he gasped a week later.

In his best impression of the outraged old witch, who Sophie's character was fighting off in this remake of *Hansel and Gretel*.

"I do dare," she said, lifting her chin. "I *do* dare, when you seek to unleash your evil on the world." Then she picked up the ruler and basket they'd been pretending were a bow and arrow and vanquished the evil witch.

He attempted to die slowly and painfully as the script called for.

And by the end of his thralls, after he'd finally gone still and groaned his last groan, he and Soph were in absolute stitches.

Which was fine by him because it meant that he could snag her around the waist, draw her close, and taste her laughter on his tongue.

Somehow, they ended up on the floor, with Soph on top of him, her hands on his shoulders, and her legs straddling his hips.

Which put his cock exactly where he preferred it—between her thighs.

She tore her shirt over her head, tossed it to the side.

"Does this mean we're done practicing your lines?" he asked, trailing his knuckles down her throat.

"I was thinking about practicing something else."

"Yeah?"

A nip to his jaw, his ear, his throat. "Yes."

"What, Tempest?"

"Why do you call me that?"

His hands clamped onto her thighs. "Tempest?"

Her tongue darted out and tasted his lips. "Yes, obviously."

He trailed his palms up and down the sensual curves of her ass, her hips, tracing them up her sides, stopping just beneath her breasts. "This bra should be illegal," he murmured, using his pointer finger to outline the black lace number, as he plotted the best way to remove the contraption, considering he couldn't see any hooks or buttons. Just crisscrossing black bands and lace cupping her luscious breasts, drawing the globes up and together and making him desperate to bury his face there.

So he did.

Kissing the inside of each breast, using his nose to nudge the straps out of the way so he could get to the treasure hidden within.

Or perhaps the treasure *beneath* was more apt.

Either way, he had to reach the hard peak that was straining through the lace, desperate for his mouth, his tongue, his teeth. So close, so close—*there*. And her moan when he sucked her nipple deep, the way her hands were kneading at his shoulders, drawing him to her, urging him on was fucking nirvana.

Except, it wasn't nirvana when he found himself stuck amongst the straps of her bra, hair caught on some piece, ear on another.

Soph moaned and gathered him close when he froze.

"Why did you stop?" she asked.

His nose was pressed against her soft skin, her scent soaking into his pores. "I'm stuck," he said, unable to stop himself from pressing a kiss to the underside of her breast.

"What?" she asked, breath catching when his lips worked on her flesh.

"I'm stuck," he said again, and again it was barely discernable, sounding more akin to *"Shim shuck"* than the reality of his words.

"What?" she repeated.

He tried to pull back but couldn't, and this time she must have realized his predicament because she exclaimed, "Oh my God. You're stuck."

The only thing he could manage was a tiny nod.

She started giggling.

"It's not funny," he grumbled. Except, it sounded like *"Shits snot shunny."*

Giggles erupted into full-blown laughter, which felt quite lovely, since it had the result of bringing her breasts against his face. The only difficulty was that he was stuck and couldn't lavish them with the attention he wanted.

The material grew tighter, her laughter still tinkling through the air, and she wiggled against him.

Then the lace loosened, coming free from her body.

He managed to unhook it from his ear, but it was firmly entrenched in his hair. "This thing is a menace."

Her lips twitched, eyes dancing with mirth. "I've had my fair share of men try to get me out of my bra."

He growled, not because of the bra, but because he couldn't bear the idea of her with anyone else.

That lip twitch grew into a full-blown smile. "Not literally, of course. Just in the proverbial trying-to-get-in-my-pants sense."

Her expression went serious. "The truth is I've never trusted anyone but you to see me completely naked. Until you." That possessive part of him settled, especially when she smiled down at him and cupped his cheek. "I've never trusted anyone like I trust you, but this particular maneuver of yours takes the cake."

Then her hand slipped away, her fingers working at the hook stuck in his hair.

A moment later he was free, and he'd shifted them, pinning her to the carpet beneath him. "You're beautiful."

She moaned when he bent and lavished her breasts with the attention he'd been desperate to give while entrapped in the evil bear trap that was the contraption of black lace and bands.

But when he moved back up to take her lips, she pressed a finger to his, stretching up to whisper in his ear. "So know, you're the only one I've been comfortable enough with to be charmed—or tangled—out of my lingerie." He grinned as her eyes came back to his, but her next words slayed him. "And you're the only one who's seen *all* of me—inside and out."

Heart thumping, he peeled her finger away from his lips. "I love you, Soph."

She froze, arms going limp to *thump* down on the carpet.

Oh, shit. He'd broken her.

He began to shift his weight off her, had opened his mouth to . . . what? Not apologize. No fucking way. He wanted her to know how he felt about her, needed her to understand this wasn't something short term, especially with her leaving in a week.

But before the words—whatever they might have turned out to be—could emerge, she was reaching for him, eyes glittering with tears.

"Rob," she whispered. "I—"

"Don't," he told her. "You don't have to say anything. I didn't tell you to rush you or—"

"I love you."

His mouth dropped open. "What?"

*Her* mouth curved up. "I love you, Rob Hansen. I never thought it would be possible to have someone like you in my life, and I certainly never expected to find a wonderful man like you while I was on vacation." Her breathing hitched. "But you helped me see *me,* and in return, you gave me you, and . . . I love you. *God,* how I love you."

How was it possible to feel this much?

Love bursting out of him making him feel like he was floating up to the sky, emotion and care for this woman tying him back down to Earth.

And desire.

Drawing his mouth back to hers, his body over hers, and long moments later, *inside* of hers. They fit perfectly and that utter sense of rightness swelled within him again, filling him up, until it exploded outward.

Until she exploded right alongside him.

---

"UGH," Soph muttered, tossing the knitting onto the table on her deck.

"Trouble?" he asked, coming out of the house, two mugs of tea in his hand.

"Yes." She shoved the knitting to the side, made a face.

Smiling at the grumpy expression, he set the mugs on the table, scooped her up into his arms, and set her on the railing of the deck. Then he stepped between her thighs and kissed her until her eyes went soft. "What's the problem?"

She sighed. "Nothing, I'm just being ridiculous."

He lifted one brow. "Why are you being ridiculous?"

Silence, her lips mutinously flat.

"Tempest," he warned.

"You never did tell me why you call me that."

"I didn't?" A brush of his fingers over her cheek, her jaw, down her throat, her scent drawing him close. "God, I love the way you smell."

"Rob," she grumbled, though her fingers clenched in his hair when he tasted the sensitive spot behind her ear.

"I call you Tempest because you swept into my life like a storm," he said, pulling back, so he could meet her eyes. "You wrecked me utterly, devastated me like a ship trapped in the middle of a hurricane." Her face clouded. "Not in a bad way, sweetheart. But in the absolute *best* way. I needed that storm, I needed to be swept from shore and out into the sea, out into the land of the living, because until I met you, I was just merely existing."

Breath shuddering out, she whispered his name again.

"But then you came along and tried to run me over"—her brows drew together in a mock-glare, though her eyes were twinkling—"and you brought me tea, and you gave me the strength to jump into that ocean, rather than just be swept along by the winds."

Her hand lifted to his cheek, cupping it. "So, the key to your heart was nearly running you over and bringing you tea?"

He grinned, smoothed his hand over the silk of her hair. "Precisely."

"I love you," she whispered, and fuck if his heart didn't skip a beat every time she said that.

The waves crashed in the background, the sky grew dark overhead, stars glimmering in the distance, and the fog crawling in. It was beautiful, but not as gorgeous as the woman in front of him. Nothing could compare to her courage, to her warmth, to her bruised and battered and somehow whole heart. "I love you." Salt in the air, the sweet scent of her in his nose. "Now, tell me why you say you're being ridiculous."

Her eyes filled with tears. "I don't want to go."

His heart skipped another beat. No, it skipped several beats as it squeezed tightly. "I don't want you to go, either," he said. "But we'll talk as often as we can, and"—he laced their fingers together—"you'll visit when you get a break."

"Which will be in forever," she moaned. "I have all of these shoots scheduled and then promotions. We'll be lucky to get a couple days together a month, maybe even less, since my house is in L.A. and—"

"So, move here."

Her mouth opened and closed. "*What?*"

Earnest now, he drew her off the railing and into his arms. "Stay with me, *move* in with me. Or if that's too much too soon, then rent a place of your own." He tucked a strand of hair behind her ear. "I'd offer to sell the business, to move to where you are, but it doesn't seem like you'll be in your house all that much anyway, and—"

"No," she said. "I would never ask that of you."

"Then make Stoneybrook your home. Come home to me, to this town when you have a break," he said, the words heartfelt. He wanted her here. Forever.

"But . . ." She bit her bottom lip.

Gently, he released that lip from the prison of her teeth. "If you want to make the most of our time together, then make a place for yourself in this town. They'd welcome you. *I'd* welcome you."

"I—um . . ." Her gaze darted away from his, and he could see her pulse pounding in her throat. "It's not that I don't want to," she whispered. "I just . . ."

Shit. She was near panic.

He needed to back off, to tread carefully.

"Just think about it, Tempest," he said. "There's no pressure. I want you here, of course. I want to spend as much time together as possible. But it's your choice, honey. Just know you have options, okay?"

She nodded, eyes still not meeting his, and he kicked himself for pushing. They'd both made leaps and bounds in the last month, had pushed beyond many barriers of their past. But he knew that she didn't have his personality, just as he knew that his brain was such that once he'd made his mind up on something, he didn't let it go. A dog to a bone. Focused and set on his course.

He was the ship navigating the tempest, bringing it safely to shore.

He *would* find a way to keep them together.

But she was still cautious, and rightfully so. They were new, not even a month old, and this was a big change for both of them, there were bound to be growing pains and fears. Which meant he needed to tread carefully.

Push, but in slow, steady increments.

"Come on," he said, stepping back and picking up her knitting from the table. "I'll show you this stitch again"—she'd begun a new project—"and then I'll let you choose what we watch tonight."

She relaxed, drifted toward him. "Even if it's *Star Trek*?"

Groaning good-naturedly, he snagged the mugs of tea then led the way back into her rental.

"Even if it's *Star Trek*, Tempest."

He could be a patient navigator through the storm.

Especially when he knew that the destination would be worth it in the end.

He just had to believe that he could coax her to come along with him.

# TWENTY-FOUR
## WALLS CLOSING IN

Soph

SHE SIGHED IN PLEASURE, the sand shifting between her toes, the breeze blowing through her hair, feeling absolutely content.

And absolutely miserable, seeing as she was leaving in two days.

Why had she agreed to do this film?

She should have cried off, pretended to never know anything about acting, and imagined she was on vacation. Permanently. Or maybe she could change careers and just become a small-town girl with small-town dreams. Have a family. Friends. Peace. Maybe open a tiny bookshop downtown.

Or maybe a wine *and* bookstore.

With equal parts of each.

Yeah, that was the perfect business model.

But, unfortunately, she couldn't cry off the movie. Not only because she'd promised to make this film, but because it was written in her contract—or at least, there was a clause in her contract that made her financially responsible if the studio wasn't willing to let her go.

And considering she was the headliner, she didn't think they would be happy for her to jump ship, especially so close to the start of shooting.

But the hardest part was that this was just the beginning of her crazy schedule, of all those back-to-back productions without a break, and then cramming publicity somewhere into the mix, finding time during those breaks-that-weren't-really-a-break because she was supposed to be learning her next script or taking classes to prepare for the role.

There wasn't any space for anyone else in her life.

Because she'd made it so.

Because she'd preferred it that way.

It was just . . . not anymore, not since this town, not since Rob, not since she'd finally found a way to be happy without her past drawing her down.

Now she worried that it would be short-lived, that she would drift back into her old patterns, that she would lose the happy, lose Rob, lose the peace she'd found in this little town.

And the thought of that trifecta disappearing made her beyond sad.

So sad, in fact, that she'd struggled to hold on to the three during her last few days here.

So, why hadn't she jumped at Rob's offer to move in with him?

She didn't want to go, didn't want to leave him or this town. And she'd all but run screaming from his offer to make something permanent. For the first time in her life she loved someone, and he loved her back, and the relationship was healthy and fulfilling.

And she'd panicked when he'd wanted to make it more.

Why?

Why, when she'd pushed through all the rest of it, was she petrified to make that final step?

Because that would make it real.

Her breath caught, knowing that was the underlying fear. Because if she made plans with Rob, figured out their future together . . . then it would no longer be this fantasy.

And she might fuck it up.

"You don't have to go, you know," Finn said, startling her out of her thoughts, reminding her that she was supposed to be spending time with her friend, with Shannon and Rylie, and not morosely pondering all the ways she was sure to mess this thing up with Rob, how she was going to miss Finn and company, along with this magical little town.

"I have to work," she told him, clinging to the convenient excuse.

Finn stopped, drawing her to a halt, the basket of sandwiches she'd brought to share swinging on her arm.

"Look," he said, nodding toward Shannon and Rylie as they played in the surf. "And ask yourself if that's *really* true."

She paused, heart thudding in her throat.

"I know you don't need the money," he said, smiling at her. "Especially since you're using the financial guy I set you up with, and aside from those heels"—his eyes went to the pair of strappy and obscenely expensive sandals dangling from her fingers—"you don't spend your money. So, if it's a work thing, you're set. You'll be able to pick your projects, to make sure your time away is only for something you feel passionate about."

"I—" She shook her head. "You make it sound so easy."

"It *is* easy." Finn nodded at his little family. "I made a decision. I made them and my life here my number one priority, and I've never regretted it or looked back." He tugged a lock of her hair. "When you find someone who fits you, who fills in the cracks and helps you grow instead of burying you deeply beneath the shit, you grab on to that person." His eyes fixed onto hers. "Whether it's a friend *or* a lover."

Her breath caught. "I'm not sure I'll ever be like you."

But that was an easy excuse, and she knew it. Because she *was* like Finn—at least in this one small way. She'd found the courage to step away from her past because she'd decided to take a chance with Rob.

"Shan's pregnant."

Soph's eyes flew to the horizon, to the lovely woman who had so thoroughly stolen Finn's heart. "Congratulations," she said. "I'm so happy for you."

"You can have your own happy, too," he said. "And you *deserve* to have it."

"Dad!" Rylie shouted, running toward them. "Look at this shell I found."

Finn smiled, moving toward her, but before the tiny tornado of energy reached them, he glanced back over his shoulder. "Grab on, Soph. Grab on tight when you've found that person and don't let go."

Her lips parted, words on the tip of her tongue, but she didn't get them out because Rylie closed the distance between her and her dad, wrapping her arms around his waist and knocking him back a pace. Finn smiled down at her.

"Hi, sunshine," he said to his daughter before looking over Ry's head and meeting Sophie's gaze, voice soft but firm. "Take that chance, and I promise you won't regret it."

She didn't get a chance to reply because he was swept away into conversation with Rylie about her seashell, but she didn't have to. Because she heard his reply to whatever words she might have summoned in her head.

*"Put your fear aside and take that chance,"* he would say. *"Because the one thing you will absolutely regret is not doing it."*

As she watched the little group at the shoreline, watched

her friend enveloped in the happiness of his family, in their love for him in return, she knew she wanted *that*. So badly, the longing was a sharp spike in her heart.

And she'd only ever wanted it with one person.

Finn swooped Rylie in the air and ran through the waves, Shannon laughing behind them as she snapped pictures with her cell. They were a family. They'd found their way.

That fear gripping her disappeared.

Because she knew she could have that—if only she found the courage.

"I'm going to fucking find the courage," she whispered. "I'm going to do it."

Dropping the basket of sandwiches to the sand, she turned away from the shore and hurried back to her cottage to get her car keys.

She needed to talk to Rob.

## TWENTY-FIVE
## UNLOCKED DOORS PART THREE

Rob

HE FINISHED MOWING THE LAWN—A task he hated with the passion of replacing sewer lines. But it was a task that needed to be done, so he'd done it.

Glamorous life.

No wonder Soph hadn't jumped into moving in with him.

She probably wanted to live somewhere bigger and more luxurious. Or maybe with a gate to keep the persistent fans out.

Not that she'd given him any indication of not liking his place.

In fact, nonstop heels aside, she fit right in with the vibe of Stoneybrook. Calm and chill and sweet. She liked being here with him and in the town. Her resistance must have come from being surprised by his offer—or perhaps, *plea* was a better term. Either way, he knew that if he were just patient and persistent, they would find a way to their future together.

Because he loved her too much to let something like an intense work schedule drive them apart.

But in the back of his mind was a kernel of insecurity.

Would he be able to convince her to give them time? Or when she went back to her real life, would she move on?

Funny how he'd been so confident, able to ignore any uncertainty so long as he didn't actually put it into words or into thoughts anyway. But giving it substance made that worry somehow grow larger.

He was working on filing that concern away, to hold tight to the confidence that he and Soph would sort things out, when he heard his name.

"Rob?"

He spun, saw someone he hadn't expected to see, someone he hadn't seen in months.

"Claudia," he said, moving toward her and starting to give her a hug before remembering he was sweaty and covered in grass. He stopped. "Sorry, I'm gross."

Carmella's mom smiled and patted him on the cheek. "You're not gross, baby."

Pretending to sniff under his arm and wincing, he said, "Want to come inside? I'll quickly clean up—unless you need me to fix something?" Claudia and Tom, Carmella's parents, had moved to the next town over about six months before, downsizing into a smaller condo with less maintenance. "Is your sink giving you trouble again?"

"No, it's not that," Claudia said, her expression concerned.

"Is something wrong?"

"No. I—" She sighed. "Can we sit down somewhere and talk?"

"Of course," he told her, leading her into the house, into the kitchen so he could at least wash the grass remnants from his hands. Then he sat down on the barstool next to her and asked, "Can I get you something to drink?"

She shook her head, wringing her hands. "No. Thanks."

Well, clearly, she had something on her mind, but he'd

learned during his years with Carmella that she couldn't be rushed, that sometimes she needed time to get her thoughts together.

So, he gave her time.

Eventually, she sighed again and managed to wrench her gaze up from his hands to his face. "I heard you're seeing someone."

His gut knotted.

That was not what he'd expected her to say. No freaking way.

"I am," he said, carefully.

Her hand covered his, squeezed lightly. "I'm happy for you," she said softly. "Truly, I am."

"So, why do you look like you swallowed a lemon?"

Bottom lip trembling, she shook her head. "It's not fair," she whispered. "Not to you, and not to Carmella. My baby wouldn't have wanted you to be alone. She loved you so much, would have wanted you to be with someone who did the same. It's just . . ." A tear streaked down her cheek.

He reached for their interlaced hands, cupped hers in both of his. "It feels more real."

A nod. "Like she's really gone." Another tear joined the first. Then more. "It's silly because she's been gone for two years now, and it shouldn't be hitting me like this. But it's like seeing you moving on makes it real all over again." Using her free hand, she dashed away the tears. "I'm so thrilled you found someone. I *am*—"

Her tears were coming in earnest now, so Rob released her hand and circled the island to retrieve the box of tissues he'd kept there . . .

Well, ever since Carmella had begun keeping them there.

Heart aching, he crossed over to Claudia, placed the box in front of her, pulling out a few and handing them to her, so she could dab her eyes. She'd been his second mom for so long that it absolutely killed him to see her this upset.

Kneeling in front of her, he waited until she looked at him. "There isn't a day that goes by that I don't miss Carmella." He shook his head, throat burning. "I'll drive through town and see the park we used to play at or go to the beach and remember all the stolen kisses."

Claudia met his eyes, her own pair narrowed. "I knew you two used to be up to no good during 'homework time.'"

He grinned. "That's true," he agreed. "But we were also up to a lot of good. So much good that sometimes my heart aches from the memory of it—even when I'm with someone new."

"Oh, baby," she murmured.

"I don't think that will ever go away. How much I loved her will never fade, and no matter who I am with now, there will never be another Carmella. She was just . . . too big, lived too fully, was too open and joyful and full of love." He patted her knee. "And because of that, your daughter will always live in my heart."

He heard a *click*, drawing his eyes to the hall, but then Claudia began crying again, this time even harder, so he didn't get up to investigate. Instead, he rose to his feet and hugged his second mom tight.

"I'll never forget Carmella," he said when she pulled back to wipe her eyes again. "I promise."

Claudia's expression gentled. "I know, baby. But I meant it when I said that I'm happy for you." She blotted her face then sighed and physically shook herself. "I came today not to have a meltdown—and I'm sorry to subject you to that—but because the rumors finally crossed town lines, and I heard you were seeing someone."

"I am."

"And from the way your eyes look right now, she's something special." Claudia patted his hand. "Now, you owe this second mom of yours all the details. Tell me about her."

An order.

And perhaps one that should have made him uncomfortable, given that this was the mother of the first woman he'd loved, but Claudia had been in his life forever, and since his mom wasn't around any longer, it felt right to share the details. "For a long time, I didn't think my heart would ever heal from the void Carmella left behind," he admitted. "But then I met Sophie."

"Sophie is a pretty name."

He smiled. "She's pretty, too. Gorgeous actually, but it's like she has this light inside her—even though she's been through some really dark and painful things, that light is still there."

"Like Carmella. The light, I mean," Claudia whispered.

"And she's got a mouth like Carmella, too." His chuckle rumbled out of his chest. "The first time we met, she nearly ran me over with her car—"

"*What?*"

He waved her off. "Long story, but suffice to say, it was my fault for being in the road. And anyway, she helped me *and* cursed me out during the process."

Claudia giggled. "That does sound like my daughter."

"But she's different in other ways," he said, wanting to reassure her and himself that he hadn't just gravitated toward Soph because he'd been looking for a replacement. "She can be so quiet, so still, happy to be sitting in a room without having to fill it with activity." Carmella had been busy, always needing to do something or to be somewhere. "She likes wine, hates beer— IPAs in particular."

Claudia's mouth twitched.

"But she's more than the similarities and differences. She's special and wonderful and . . . my heart feels complete when I'm with her."

A sniff.

"I'm sorry," he said quickly. "I didn't mean to—"

"No. That's not why I'm crying, honey." She grabbed another tissue and blew her nose. "You know I'm a watering pot on a normal day." She used her free hand to cover his again. "I wish you every bit of happiness, Rob. I'm so glad to see you living again, and I want you to keep doing it." She sniffed. "Live your life big, baby. Live it to its fullest and don't ever look back. Not *ever*."

Now his eyes stung, tears clogging the back of his throat. "Claud," he whispered.

"Come here and give me another gross, sweaty hug."

He stood and obliged her then they spent a few minutes catching up on non-heavy things before she ordered him to shower while she saw herself out, so he could go see *his* Soph.

Then with a wave, she disappeared into the hall, the front door *clicking* shut behind her.

But he didn't pay attention to the noise.

He was too excited to get to Soph.

# TWENTY-SIX
## PACKED BAGS

Soph

SHE WAS DYING.

Literally felt as though her heart had been torn from her body and she'd crunched it beneath her high-heeled sandals.

And she couldn't even blame anyone.

Not Rob. Not herself.

Not the ghost of a woman he still loved.

She'd known Carmella was there, had wholly accepted that she would always be part of Rob's heart because of the depth of their love.

She'd just thought . . . there was room for her.

*How much I loved her will never fade, and no matter who I am with now, there will never be another Carmella.*

She hadn't wanted to be another Carmella, but now she saw that she would never even come close. Rob might think he loved her, Rob might care about her, but she would never occupy the same space.

"That's okay," she tried to tell herself as she drove home, crawling through the streets at a snail's pace, worried that she was so scattered she might lose focus and really hit someone. "It's okay to not be the same as her."

Soph could occupy a different space.

But would it ever come close to what he had with Carmella? Would she love this man with every fiber of her being and not ever be held deeply in his heart?

Oh, he wouldn't do it intentionally. He was too nice of a guy to do that, to treat her as second best. It was just . . . she would always know she was.

"Fuck," she hissed, pulling into the garage at the rental and resting her head on the steering wheel. Her eyes burned with tears even though she was desperately trying to be logical about this. Clearly, whoever had been in the house had cared deeply about Rob's late wife. He was probably trying to reassure them. He was probably just making sure they were okay.

But all she could think was how he'd sounded when he said, *No matter who I am with now, there will never be another Carmella.*

And *Soph* was who he was with.

All of those old feelings, all the heavy shit she'd thought she was finally over, everything she'd hoped was buried and gone forever . . . all of it washed over her, sitting on her heart, her lungs. And she knew, despite what she'd thought over the last month, she would never be good and pure like Carmella. She would never be what Rob deserved, not when he deserved the world.

Her heart had been dropped into a whirling blender, and she hadn't thought it was possible to be in this much pain when there was nothing actually physically wrong with her.

Perhaps, it was better to learn this now, with her leaving.

It was the perfect punctuation mark.

She'd started empty. She'd found more. And she'd leave empty, all over again.

They could just both forget everything and go back to normal. Normal. *Yes.* Desperate for the cold nothingness, the even numbness, she grasped on to normal, to things going back to the way they were before.

The knock on her window made her jump and glance up.

And want to crawl under the tires of a moving car.

Rob was smiling in at her, hand still lifted from the knock, but one look had his face filling with concern and reaching for the door handle.

"Soph," he said, once the door was open. "What's wrong?"

And she knew she had a decision to make.

Was she going to get into a giant confrontation with him, was she going to admit she'd heard what she'd heard, that she'd heard how he truly felt? Listen to him convince her—and himself in the process—that what they had was different but no less valuable. He would certainly tell her that, certainly even believe it himself. But *she* wasn't going to believe him. She *couldn't* afford to believe him. Not when so much was at stake.

So . . . instead of an argument, she was going to soak in this last sliver of time with the man whom she loved quite desperately. She was going to avoid ending their interlude with tears and recriminations.

She would hold on to the good memories and give herself one more chance at a few more.

The decision was the easiest of her life.

Unbuckling her seat belt, she pushed out of her seat and wrapped her arms around his shoulders and told her first lie to this man.

"I'm okay," she said, putting her acting skills to use. "It's just . . . I have to fly out tomorrow instead of the next day, and I'm so freaking disappointed."

Cursing, he pulled back, eyes filled with disappointment. "Me, too, Tempest."

*Slice.* The endearment sliced right through her heart. She forced a smile.

His fingers trailed the shape of it. "What time is your flight?"

"Nine in the morning."

He hissed out a breath, lips pressing flat. "Damn, that sucks." He shifted, cupped her cheek. "But I guess that's what I get for dating a famous woman." Rob smiled, lightly stroking his thumb across her skin. "Can I drive you to the airport?"

She should have said no, but instead, some perverse part of her wanted to soak in every last drop of him. "Yes," she said, "I'd like that."

"You probably need to pack, huh?"

Yes, she did.

She also needed to book a flight—or have her assistant do it, anyway.

"Okay, here's what we'll do. I'll go grab a pizza and a change of clothes then we'll come back and pack up the cottage. Work for you?"

"Rob, you don't have—" she began.

"I don't *have* to do anything," he said. "But what I *want* is to spend every possible second with you between now and when you leave, even if that involves folding your skivvies."

Even with her heart in shreds, the man still made her laugh.

"Okay?" he asked.

She nodded. "Okay, honey."

He kissed her briefly then turned toward his truck.

"Rob?"

He spun back to face her.

"I love you."

His smile touched all the dark and jagged places inside her. "I love you, too, Tempest."

Then he was gone, getting into his truck and driving away

while she moved into the cottage, made a call to her assistant to arrange the nine o'clock flight and accommodations upon her arrival in Italy.

She'd finished packing her clothes by the time he returned with the pizza—Hawaiian for her, pepperoni for him—and over slices, he made plans for her return, jotting down dates in the calendar on his phone.

"You'll stay at my place in between shoots?" he asked.

Heartsick, she just nodded, knowing there was no way she'd ever allow herself to come back here.

"Then you'll fly out to Hungary a week later?"

Another nod. "As long as everything stays on schedule."

He made another note on his phone.

"And then—"

She couldn't listen to anymore, not knowing what she knew, not knowing what she *needed* to do. Leaning across the table, she kissed him.

"Soph," he said, tearing his mouth away after a long, hot kiss. "We should talk—"

"I need you, Rob," she murmured. "Please. It's our last night together."

His eyes dimmed, and he pushed out of the chair, scooping her up and carrying her down the hall. He set her gently on the bed and tugged off her heels. "Our last night, just for a while," he said, pressing a kiss to her ankle.

She couldn't bring herself to agree.

Instead, she wound her fingers into his hair and tugged him up then she kissed him with every ounce of love she had for this man. She would soak up this moment, this night, this fantasy, and hold tight to it for the remainder of her life.

Because as the sun set, as he stripped her clothes and worshipped every inch of her skin, she knew that she would never set foot in Stoneybrook again.

Her heart was broken.

But it would heal—or if not heal, then eventually, she would find her way back to the perfect numbness.

Her life would go back to normal.

And so would Rob's.

Which was the only way she found the strength not to cry the next morning when he drove her to the airport, parked at the private tarmac where her plane would fly out, and handed her a box.

"Open it," he whispered.

She tugged the lid off and . . . almost lost her battle with tears.

Inside was the purple sweater she'd so admired in the window of Misty's shop all those weeks before.

"How?" she whispered.

"Misty owed me a favor."

"I—I—" Battle lost; a tear slid down her cheek.

He pulled the sweater from the box and handed it to her. "Wear it to keep you warm on those cold nights without me, okay?"

Her nod was jerky, and she wiped her eyes, holding back the rest of the tears by pure stubbornness—or perhaps, it was the numbness washing over her again. Weighing her down, making her cold.

She grasped on to the sweater, held it to her chest.

And then she allowed herself one more kiss, one more long, scorching bit of contact to feed her soul.

She got out of Rob's truck.

He got out, too, retrieving her suitcase from the back and handing it to the steward, who'd come down to check her documents.

Then it was time to get on the plane.

"Rob," she whispered.

"Hush, now, Tempest," he said, enfolding her in his arms. "Don't worry, I'll make sure your rental car gets back to the lot." He tapped her on the nose. "Without running anyone over, I promise."

More laughter.

More kisses.

More heart-shattering.

Then, clutching that beautiful sweater to her chest, she said goodbye and got on the fucking plane.

# TWENTY-SEVEN
## SILENCE

Rob

HE'D THOUGHT something was wrong the moment that Soph had announced she was leaving on an earlier flight than planned.

But he'd been off his game after the conversation with Claudia then blindsided by the news of Soph's departure.

Now, however, as the days had gone on, as she hadn't returned his calls or texts or emails, he'd realized his error.

She wasn't upset about her departure—or not *just* that. She was upset because she was ending them.

Or maybe she wasn't upset so much as trying to scrape him off.

That kernel of doubt had turned into a boulder.

Maybe this entire thing was some sick acting ploy, some way to poke fun at the sad little small-town widower. Maybe—

*That* was the bullshit talking.

Soph was a hell of an actress, but she certainly wasn't malicious and what she'd shared, the care and loveliness that she'd given him . . . no, he couldn't believe that was all fake.

He couldn't.

Which meant he needed to find a way to her.

Which meant . . . he needed Finn.

Luckily enough, he knew where the man lived.

Knocking on his door, Rob paced back and forth, waiting for Finn to answer it. Then knocking again when he didn't. The lights were on inside, and he could smell the beginnings of dinner. They were home, and he needed to talk to his friend, and he'd keep pounding on the door until, finally, after long moments and a third knock, Finn *did* come to the door, his T-shirt on inside out, his hair a fucking disaster, and his jeans not completely buttoned.

"What?" he growled, making it clear why it had taken the course of three knocks.

Rob didn't care what he'd interrupted.

He needed to get to Soph.

Not wasting any time, Rob explained the situation ending with a plea, plain and simple. "I need your help."

Finn's face had grown more serious throughout Rob's entire speech. "Are you sure she wants you?"

As far as blows went, that was a heavy one.

"No," he said, "I don't know that, at least not a hundred percent. I hope she does. What we shared . . ." Fuck. "What we shared was . . . *more*, Finn. It was . . . not a fantasy or a fling. It was important and big and *fuck*, it was a glimpse of my future." Spinning, he thrust a hand through his hair. "And she's not running now because she's doesn't want me or us. She's running because she's terrified of wanting us, of wanting more, of what that *more* might mean."

He broke off, heart beating rapidly, breaths sawing through him.

And Finn was silent, just staring at him.

For endless minutes.

Then finally, Finn nodded. "Go home and pack a bag then get your ass to the airport."

Relief poured through him, and he turned for his truck.

"Hey, Rob?"

He stopped, glanced back.

"Do you have a passport?"

Brows drawing together, he asked, "Yeah, why?"

"Because you're going to Italy."

# TWENTY-EIGHT
# THE SWEATER

Soph

EXHAUSTION MADE her limbs heavy as the elevator doors dinged open and she stumbled her way down the hall to her room.

The air was cool this late autumn evening, and she could think of nothing more than a long, hot bath, washing her face free of the on-camera makeup she wore, cuddling up in Rob's sweater, and basking in her misery.

It had been more than a week without talking to him, and she felt as though she'd lost a limb.

She was starting to think that she'd made a mistake.

No, she'd *known* she'd made a mistake.

But did she have the courage to right it? Her stomach twisted itself into knots, just considering it.

The only positive was that her character was as morose as they came, and for once, she didn't have to actually act. Instead, she was just her miserable self, parroting her lines to the camera.

And somehow, this wreck of a *Hansel and Gretel* remake might actually not turn out half-bad.

Snorting over the very unlikeliness of that statement, she let herself into her room. Immediately, her eyes went to the bed, neatly made, the purple sweater spread out on the comforter near its foot, and all at once, it became too much.

She was such an idiot.

She should have just told Rob what she had heard, how it had made her feel, how in that moment, she had known that he was too good for her, that she was unworthy of love in the same vein as his late wife.

He might have convinced her differently.

He might have made her feel worthy.

He might—

Her blood froze in her veins.

Her eyes slid closed as she sank to the carpet, just inside the room, her back resting against the door, her head on her knees.

Because why did she continue to look for worth in other people?

"Why?" she whispered. Why could she not find that worth in herself?

God, was *this* really going to be how she lived the rest of her life? Miserable and alone and constantly feeling as though she were not enough.

For once, she wanted to look into herself and . . . be happy with what she saw.

But *how* did one go about doing that?

How did some people just live their lives with confidence and not find themselves lacking or weighed down by their past?

Every time she thought she was beyond what had been done to her, how it had made her feel, every time she thought she'd shrugged off the burden of that heavy weight, Soph remembered how she'd felt afterward.

Dirty and used and washed up.

Broken and lost and trampled upon.

Sighing, she moved to the bathroom, washing her face, removing the false lashes, and then finally just staring at herself in the mirror.

"How have you gotten here?" she whispered, touching a finger to her reflection.

She knew she should be proud. She'd pieced her life together, found a way to stability, in a career that most people would give their right arm to be part of. Money, fame, success. She had them all.

But she wasn't happy.

In fact, the only time she *had* been happy was when she was with Rob.

*No.* That wasn't entirely true.

She'd been happy with him *and* the entire time she was in Stoneybrook.

Because . . . she'd allowed herself to be more than her past, more than the scars and the things that had been done to her. She'd been more than the numbness and fear and living life in a bubble.

Free.

She'd been free.

"And now I'm trapped again," she whispered. Trapped and miserable and all the more so because she knew what it was to be happy and loved and—

"Ugh!"

Slamming her hands down on the counter, she left the bathroom, grabbed the sweater, and yanked it over her head. If she was going to be trapped and miserable and lonely, she might as well be warm and comfortable.

Just as she'd tugged the sweater over her head, her phone rang.

Heart pounding, she swiped a finger across the screen and

lifted it to her ear, not daring to look at the number, not wanting to shatter the hope that it was Rob calling.

She'd ignored his calls for a week, and now all she wanted was to hear his voice.

But that was not to be.

Because when she said, "Hello?" it wasn't Rob's voice that answered her.

"Peanut."

"Ben," she said with a smile, all the stress and angst she'd been whipping to a frenzy inside her settling with just that one nickname.

"How's my favorite daughter?" he asked.

"Adopted daughter," she told him, smiling at the memory. He was the agent who'd saved her from the hellhole her father had sold her into, the one who'd brought her into his home and helped her heal.

A sigh. "*Favorite* daughter," he said, in his normal no-nonsense voice.

The one that had dared her to argue about that fact over the years, and the one that told her she wouldn't win this argument tonight, just as she hadn't won it at any point in the last decade and a half.

"Favorite daughter," she repeated dutifully.

"That's my girl," he said, his rich voice filling her with warmth. "How are you doing?"

"I'm working." A laugh. "So, I'm doing great." Then added before he could ferret out whatever would be in her tone, because her hurricane of feelings *would* be in her tone and because Ben never failed to detect when she was off, "How was your and Martha's cruise?"

He sighed again. "Fucking cesspool."

She snorted. "Then why do you go every year?"

"Why do you think I go?" he asked.

"Martha." Her heart squeezed. "Because she loves it."

"Ding. Ding. Ding. And I was gone enough during the early years of our marriage to be happy to humor her, especially when she could have easily left my dumb ass many a time over the years." He laughed. "How was your time in that little town? Peaceful, I hope? No paparazzi I need to serve with restraining orders?"

Giggling, she shook her head, then realized—duh—that he couldn't see her. So she said, "Yes to the peace. No to the paparazzi and restraining orders."

"So why do you sound so sad?"

See what she meant about ferreting?

Stifling a sigh, she murmured, "Don't worry about it."

"I'll always worry about my favorite daughter."

"Only daughter, I feel obligated to point out," she said.

"Just because one fact is true doesn't mean the other isn't."

Soph stopped breathing as those words traveled thousands of miles through the airways then through the speaker of her cell and finally through the hair cells of her ear, moving them and shifting the tiny bones against the tympanum.

But when they finally processed in her brain, all time stood still.

Just because one thing was true, didn't mean the other wasn't.

Just because Rob had loved Carmella, didn't mean he couldn't love her, too. Just because she'd been hurt in the past didn't mean she couldn't live now.

Was it that easy?

*Could* it be that easy?

"Soph?" Ben asked, concern heavy in his tone now.

"I'm here," she told him. "I'm just . . . did Martha ever resent you bringing me home?"

A sharp inhale followed by a long silence.

Heart pounding, she waited for him to answer, waited for a response to a question she hadn't even comprehended that she'd needed answering.

"Did *you?*" she asked softly into the silence.

Another inhale, this one paired with a curse. "Are you fucking kidding me, Soph? Where are you right now? Because I'm going to get my ass on a plane so I can come shake that thought out of you." His words were rapid and clipped. "No, seriously, where are you?" he snapped when she didn't immediately answer.

"Italy," she mumbled.

"Ach," he growled. "I should have stayed in the Mediterranean. Would have been easier to get to you and smack some sense into that pretty head of yours."

"Ben," she began.

"No, Soph," he said. "Stop talking, because I'm only going to say this once, and I want to make sure you're listening."

Lips parting on a shaky exhale, she waited.

"I have never regretted bringing you home to join our family. Not *one* time," he added firmly. "Neither have Martha or the boys. From the moment you walked into our house, too fucking skinny and still healing from your injuries, but with your chin held high and your shoulders straight, none of us have *ever* had anything except for the greatest amount of love and respect for you." His voice was husky. "The only thing I regret, the *only* thing, is that I didn't get there sooner, and because of that, you suffered." He blew out a breath, tone evening out. "Well, that and also that you never really got justice, since that fucker was killed before he stood trial."

"Actually, I was always thankful for that," she whispered. "Thankful that he died, and I didn't have to stand in front of him and remember. Same as my father and mother." She swallowed the knot in her throat. "It was almost easier that they'd been killed. I didn't have to face them, to look into their eyes and remember the fate they'd thrust upon me."

"I get that, Soph," he said, "and I think anyone in your situation would feel the same as you."

She sighed. "Yeah."

"Is that why you're sad? You're remembering the past?"

"No." Her lips pressed flat, released. "Yes, I guess. It's just . . . have you ever thought you had everything in your life figured out, and then it all went topsy turvy?"

He chuckled. "Yeah, honey, I have. What's going on?"

"I—" She broke off. "I don't think I'm ready to talk about it yet, but I just . . . for so long I didn't think that I could be normal, have normal relationships, and I got really good at keeping everyone at a distance. Well, I wasn't so great at it with you Jacksons." She laughed. "I never stood a chance against the force of you and my five older, pushier brothers."

"Damn right, you didn't."

She smiled. "You guys were there for me when things were the worst, but I know I've pulled back from the family over the last few years."

"You were busy building a career."

"Yes," she murmured. "But also, it was easier."

A long pause. "Easier how?"

"Easier for me to pretend it never happened."

He inhaled sharply. "Peanut," he whispered. "I'm sorry. I didn't realize."

"How could you?" she said, or maybe croaked, her throat was so tight from bottled up tears. "I just wondered . . . fuck, not wondered, the truth is that I *still* wonder how I could possibly be of value when my father sold me."

Ben cursed, and she wished he was here, that he was wrapping her in his heavy arms, tugging her against his chest, and hugging her tight. He'd always given the best hugs.

"And I hate it," she said, tears spilling over. "I know I shouldn't feel that way, but . . ."

"Sometimes it creeps back in," he finished for her.

"Yes."

"I wish I could fight this battle for you, Peanut. I wish I could take this burden from you. I wish you wouldn't have ever been in that shitty situation and so hurt and—" Another curse. "I would give up having you in my life if I could ensure you would have had happiness."

"Ben," she whispered, wiping her tears away. "I—"

"But I can't take it away. I can't shoulder that weight." His voice cracked. "But I *can* tell you that the only way to truly get beyond the things that haunt you is to face them head on."

Her lungs froze.

"You're a fighter, Soph. You always have been," he said. "So now, here's the opportunity. You've identified what's holding you back, what's hurting you." His voice went soft but no less intense. "Fight for yourself. Fight for your happiness. Fight for your *life*."

Heart pounding, she said, "I'll try."

"Promise?"

Somehow, she smiled. "I promise."

"Good," he said. "Now, tell me about this shoot of yours. How are they treating you?"

"Same old," she told him, and they spent a few minutes catching up about her project and his cruise. She answered automatically but wasn't really processing anything that came out of her mouth. Eventually, Ben hung up after saying he would call her in a couple of days to check in on her, leaving the conversation swashing around her head like a half-filled bucket.

Fight. Just fight.

Could it really be that easy?

And yet, how could she *not* fight? How could she not? How—

"Fuck," she whispered then swapped out her heels for sneakers—sacrilege, she knew—and left her hotel room.

She should be resting, should be reviewing for tomorrow.

But all she could think was that she needed to figure out her own heart and head before she could do *any* of that. And she knew she wasn't going to figure out either in here, trapped in her hotel room.

She needed to walk and think and understand why she'd torpedoed the one good thing she'd had going in her life.

Why she hadn't bothered to fight.

And . . . if she had the strength to fight now.

---

THE NEXT DAY was a little better.

She was exhausted from her exploits the night before, well, from walking the quiet streets of the small Italian town they were filming in until almost one in the morning, but she *had* found a little slice of peace.

A narrow stream winding through an open field, babbling softly under the moonlight.

It wasn't the ocean or its waves pounding against a shoreline.

But it was a peaceful place and one that had given her time to think.

To remember . . . *everything*.

The bad and the good, the painful and not, and most of all, she'd been able to remember the girl she once had been. And she'd decided she didn't want to go back to that naïve, silly girl, the one who'd thought the world was all easy kindness and getting everything she wanted.

It wasn't that she liked holding on to what had happened to her.

No, part of her still thought it would be better off buried. But she'd tried that already, and it had made her miserable.

So, she'd decided that she didn't need to like what happened to her.

She could fucking hate it, despise the people who'd hurt her, and still love herself.

Because she could fight.

And she was going to, dammit.

For herself . . . and for Rob.

The elevator dinged, and she trudged off, heels dragging on the carpet, eyes barely open as she made her way down the hall to her room.

Which was probably why she didn't notice the person there.

Why she didn't notice the *man* standing outside her door.

Not until he'd snagged the key out of her hand, not until he'd opened the door to her room and tugged her inside, not until the scream was bubbling up out of her throat.

# TWENTY-NINE
## THE RECKONING

Rob

SHE WAS dead on her feet.

He could see that from a mile away.

At first, he'd felt a stab of pain, thinking she was ignoring him. But then he'd seen her face, the way her eyes were downcast and not processing her surroundings—later, they'd discuss *that*.

Now, they had other things to sort.

"It's me," he said, placing a finger to her lips to stymie her startled yell.

"Rob?" she whispered once he'd dropped his hand, turned back to the door, and thrown the lock.

"Yes."

He moved into the bathroom, turned on the tub.

"But how are you here?"

After checking the water temperature and plugging the basin, he turned back to Soph and herded her to the bed. "I flew." A beat as he nudged her down onto the mattress. "On a plane." He bent and tugged off her heels, chucking the sexy torture devices to the far side of the room. Damned woman looked like she'd been dragged backward through a hedge, the least she could do was wear some fucking flats.

He reached for the button on her jeans, flicked it open and yanked the zipper down then tugged the material from her legs.

Ignoring the lace and the tempting way it cupped her, he reached for her shirt.

She batted his hands away. "What are you doing?"

"You're exhausted," he said. "You're taking a bath, I'm ordering you room service, and then you're getting twelve hours of sleep."

"I have a call time in nine hours."

"Fine," he muttered. "You're getting eight and a half hours of sleep."

She scowled. "Don't give me orders."

"Then take care of yourself better."

Her scowl transformed into a glare. "I'm doing just fine, thank you."

He snorted.

She shoved him back, pushed to her feet. "I am *okay*, and I don't need . . ."

Rob went deathly still. "Me?"

She swallowed, eyes darting to the side then back to his. "No," she said, and a bolt of pain shot through him. But then she kept talking and he felt hope, so much fucking hope. "No, I *do* need you."

His lungs unstuck.

"I'm—" A shake of her head, her shoulders lifting and falling on an exhale. "I heard you in your kitchen talking to that woman about Carmella."

He closed his eyes, opened them slowly as clarity filled him. "I'm guessing you didn't stick around to listen to me talking about *you?*"

She shook her head. "No, baby, I didn't. I was a fucking idiot to not stay, to not tell you." A sigh. "But I think even without hearing that conversation, I would have run at some point anyway."

"Why?" he asked, brows drawn together.

"Because . . . I don't think I'm worthy of love." She sighed, put her hand up when he immediately began protesting that bullshit. "No, I *know* I'm worthy . . . it's just that sometimes I don't believe it, sometimes I think I'm a burden and can't give enough in return, and sometimes . . . I think it's easier to run and hide from what I want because if I don't have *anything*, then I can't be disappointed when it goes away."

His throat went tight. "Soph," he rasped.

Her shoulders straightened. Her chin lifted. "But I don't want that anymore."

He cupped her cheek.

She covered his hand with her own. "I don't want to be alone without any real friends, avoiding my family because they see too much, avoiding you because you make me *feel* too much."

She was killing him. "Soph, *baby*, stop."

"No," she whispered, a tear trailing down her cheek. "I've spent the last week alone and miserable and thinking myself into circles, wanting what I thought I couldn't have, needing more than I was willing to be open for, and . . ." She blinked, and he wiped the tear away.

"And what, Tempest?"

Her eyes opened, those pale-gray irises damp like an early morning storm.

"And . . . I'm finally ready to fight for me, for you, for *us*." Determination filled her gaze. "I love you. I want you. So I'm saying, begging, pleading, demanding"—her lips curved—"that you *choose* me. *Love* me."

Rob's heart thudded in his chest. He opened his mouth to tell her that would never be an issue, that he would always love her.

But she kept talking.

"I know, I'm still a mess. I know I'm a total dumpster fire. I know, I still have things to work through, and I could very well run or push you away again—"

"And I will come after you." He rested his forehead against hers, cutting off her words with a brief kiss. "I will come after you again and again *and* again. Because I won't let you go, Soph."

She released a shaky exhale. "But—"

"No, *buts*. I've lost too much to ever go down without a fight." He brushed his lips to hers. "Lucky I have a brand-new, not expired passport"—when her brows pulled down, he said, "I'll explain later. Suffice to say, I would have been here sooner if not for having to get it reissued. The point is that I have my passport and a friend with a private jet." He fixed her in place with a glare. "So, send me away. Run as far as you want. Just know that I'll fight for you, too."

"Rob," she whispered.

"Soph," he whispered back.

"I love you."

"I love *you*."

He kissed her, long and slow and tender, holding her close and still gently, always gently, his fingers stroking through her hair, filling her heart with affection and hope and *love* for this man and their future.

"I'm sorry I ran."

He rested his hand on the side of her neck. "I'm *not* sorry you found your fight."

She smiled. "You may regret that fight someday, especially when I'm making you watch *Star Trek* for the umpteenth time."

"Never," he said. "And speaking of that"—he stepped back from her, moved to the small duffle bag he'd brought with him, and pulled out the DVD—"I wasn't sure if this had traveled to Italy, yet."

Her lips parted, eyes warming, and he had to force himself to go back into the bathroom and turn off the water—or else risk flooding the hotel while kissing the woman he loved beyond reason again. But then the water was off, the flood avoided, and he could get back to her, could take her in his arms.

They had a foundation to continue building, practical things to work out, schedules to finesse, baggage to still work through.

But they had each other. They had their love.

Rob knew it might not always be easy, but he also knew they would be okay. Because Soph and he had both found their fight. Because they could turn to each other in the darkness. They were two souls perfectly aligned because they'd come through that hurt and pain, and they found each other on the other side.

Plus, he thought as he let his lips fall to hers again, he still had that friend with the private jet.

# EPILOGUE

## SCREECHING BRAKES

Soph, a year later

SHE SMILED as she drove along the darkened road, so happy to be back in Stoneybrook.

It had been three months since she'd been home and nearly six weeks since she'd seen Rob—both because of the remote Iceland location her latest film, a modern adaptation of *Peter Pan*, with her playing the mischievous child who never wanted to grow up, but also because he'd been slammed with work.

But now she was back, now she had a solid six months at her new home base, with only the odd break for publicity.

She'd sold her L.A. home.

She'd moved in with Rob.

And . . . she was happy.

Not perfectly happy all the time. Sometimes she still had dark moments, still had to consciously remind herself that she was worth all of the affection and love and joy that was brought into her life—by Rob, by Misty, by Ben and Martha and company, by Finn and Shann and Rylie.

But her life, her little slice of family, had grown exponentially, and she was so damned thankful for that every day.

Today, however, she wasn't thinking about her family.

She was thinking about Rob and the present she had for him.

Six weeks was a long time. Six weeks was long enough for her to—

"Shit!"

She screeched to a halt on a familiar dark stretch of road, her tires loud on the asphalt, her brakes protesting, her heart beating a mile a minute as she watched the deer slowly meander in front of her, its large antlers sharp and gleaming in the moonlight.

"Motherfucker," she muttered, turning into the driveway that had become her home. It wasn't fancy and didn't have a huge gate—though they *had* installed a state-of-the-art security system after a fan had come too close. Luckily, those interactions were rare, and the town had her back, protecting her like they shielded Finn and Pepper from the hordes of paparazzi that plagued them in other towns.

She still had her peace and quiet and this lovely house full of warmth and love and . . . Rob.

The small craftsman wasn't that gorgeous cottage she'd stayed at on the beach, she thought with a small pang of remorse. *That* home had gone on the market, and though she'd put in an offer, it had gone to someone else.

Which was fine, because *this* was home.

The garage door opened, and she pulled in, allowing it to close behind her before grabbing her purse and getting out of her car. But when she reached into the trunk for her suitcase, warm hands stopped her.

"I've got it, Tempest."

She smiled and turned into Rob's arms, noting the sleepy

eyes, the mussed hair. He must have heard the heavy garage door sliding open.

"Hi, baby," she whispered, hugging him tight.

"Hi, yourself." He kissed her forehead. "You weren't supposed to get in until tomorrow."

The bristle on his jaw caught her hair as he reached past her and pulled out her bag. "I got an earlier flight."

"Mmm." His hand rested on her hip as he nudged her toward the house. "I missed you."

"Pish," she said, flicking on the light when they walked into the kitchen and throwing herself into his embrace. "You know that you love my returning home kisses." And to put her money where her mouth was, she slanted her lips across his, kissing him deeply.

There was no hesitation, just love and happiness . . . and *heat*.

Plenty of pent-up heat that had him lifting her up onto the counter, her purse falling to the floor, and he dropped to his knees and gave her *her* favorite returning home kiss. Then he stood, spread her thighs, slid in deep, and rocked them both slowly into oblivion.

After, they sat on the kitchen floor—her in his T-shirt, him in just a pair of boxer briefs—and caught up on everything they hadn't been able to talk about over the last six weeks. She heard how Misty's bathroom remodel was finally completed—and Rob would be getting shit for an eternity about how he'd allowed his sister's project to run a *year* over schedule. He heard how she'd had a frightening scare on the ice when it had creaked ominously below everyone's feet and they all had made a quick exodus to the safety of solid ground. Then they talked about nothing—TV and movies that weren't hers, a book she was developing for production, where they wanted to travel during her time off.

It was everything she'd missed when away from him, and it still filled her heart to capacity, the love she had for this man.

"We should get some sleep," he said, much later, the sky beginning to lighten.

Nodding, she started to push to her feet, but he swept her up into his arms, carried her upstairs, and tucked her under the covers of their bed.

"Would you mind getting my purse?" she asked before he could settle in next to her. "I brought you something."

His face went soft, fingers brushing her cheek before he went back downstairs.

A moment later, he'd returned with the black bag in one hand, her suitcase in the other.

She took the purse while he stowed her luggage in the corner of the room then came over to the bed and snuggled close and she retrieved the small, wrapped box. "Present, please," he said, kissing her neck.

"Impatient?" she asked, arching her brow.

"Presents are my favorite," he teased, taking the box when she held it out. "But seriously"—he cupped her cheek—"I missed you, Tempest."

She smiled, pressed a kiss to his lips, before breaking away and nodding at the box. "Open it already."

Grinning, he tore off the paper, tossing it to the side, then opened the lid.

And froze.

She nibbled at her lip, waiting as he processed what was inside, since she'd had very much the same reaction when she'd found out.

His eyes, warm tiger's eyes came to hers. "Is this . . ."

Soph nodded.

He dropped the box and pulled her into his chest, his arms coming tightly around her. "You're pregnant?" he asked.

"Six weeks along," she whispered. "So, it's really early. But I missed my period a couple of weeks ago and I got the test yesterday, and . . . I had to tell you in person that we're going to have a baby."

His hand came to her stomach, still flat, then to her cheek, cupping it so gently. "Baby, I'm so fucking happy. I-I—" He blinked. "We're going to have a *baby*."

"I know." She laughed, heart full. "I'm fucking terrified, but I'm also so happy."

"Me, too, Tempest. Me, too." He pulled her close, hugging her tightly, stroking his fingers through her hair in that way of his he always did. "I love you so much."

"I love *you*."

He released her. "Lay down," he said, coaxing her down on the mattress and pulling the blankets up to her chin. "How have you been feeling? Have you been sick? Do I need to go to the grocery store?"

She sat up. "Rob."

He nudged her back down. "You need your rest."

She scowled. "Are you going to try to order me around this whole pregnancy?"

"Nope." He tucked the blankets tighter. "But I *will* take care of you."

"Is taking care of me another word for ordering me around?" she asked archly.

His lips twitched. "Maybe." A wave of his hand. "We can argue about it later."

God, she loved this man. Even when he was infuriating her.

"For now." He turned for his nightstand and pulled out an envelope, handing it to her.

"What's this?"

"I had a present for you, too."

Brows pulling together, she asked, "What is it?"

"You'll find out," he said and kissed her forehead. "*If* you open it."

Since he had a point, she didn't argue. Instead, she peeled open the flap and pulled out the folded sheaf of papers inside, reading the legalese. Then *processing* the legalese.

Her mouth dropped open.

Her eyes flew to his.

"You bought—" She shook her head. "*You* bought the cottage?"

He nodded. "Turns out, I don't mind having Finn as a neighbor." His lips found hers, stealing her breath in a hot kiss. "And you wanted it, Tempest."

"Rob," she breathed, eyes stinging.

"I love you, sweetheart," he said, "and I want you to have everything you ever wanted, everything you've ever dreamed of."

Wrapping her arms around him and tugging him to her, she kissed him until her lungs burned, until she had to break away to suck in air.

"I already have it," she whispered, her forehead resting against his. "Everything I've ever dreamed of, and so much more."

---

Misty

She sat on the deck of Rob and Soph's cottage, enjoying the breeze in her hair, the sun on her skin, and the brief quiet from the party on the sand.

Soph had just announced she was pregnant.

Misty was so happy for her and her brother, so glad they'd found each other and managed to carve out a slice of fulfillment.

It was just . . . she was jealous.

So *freaking* jealous.

And add in a dash of guilt. Because her brother had barely survived the death of his first wife, had been a shell of a man for two full years until Sophie had come into the picture on her sexy little heels, with her Hollywood smile and her sweet personality.

Yup. She was a famous actress.

And she was *nice*.

Ugh.

Sighing, she sat back and lifted her glass of wine to her lips, glugging down a large sip and looking out at the surf. Of all the places to live in town, her brother certainly had picked a good one.

Even if she was a jealous, guilty asshole.

She had her own business. She'd bought a house. She'd just paid off her car. She had a full life.

A full, single, *lonely* life.

Fun, fun.

Resisting the urge to sigh again, she drained her glass then made her way over to say goodbye to her brother and Soph and the rest of the crew.

"Oh," Soph said, after she'd made her excuses. "I was hoping you might stay around. My dad and brothers are coming to visit." She checked her watch. "They're actually supposed to be here any minute."

"I have an early morning delivery," Misty lied. "I'm sorry. I really need to get to bed."

"I understand." Soph squeezed her hands. "I'll make dinner this week on a night you can join us."

She forced a smile. "That sounds great."

She waved to Finn, cradling their newest addition, high-fived Rylie, and called a goodbye to Shannon, then she hightailed it across the sand, determined to allow herself one more night of sulking before she got it together and stopped feeling so sorry for herself.

Misty had a lot going for her.

She just needed to remember that.

*Tomorrow.* After she finished the bottle of wine in her fridge and the pint of ice cream in her freezer. After she'd lit her favorite candle and soaked in her tub, consuming bad reality TV right alongside all those extra calories.

"See?" she whispered to herself as she got into her car and turned on the engine, slowly backing out of the driveway. "This will all be fi—"

*Crunch.*

Her sedan—her awesome, recently-paid off sedan—jerked to a halt.

"Fuck," she whispered, looking in her review and seeing that she'd run into a large black SUV. An SUV that currently had smoke coming from beneath the hood. She cursed again, dropping her head to the steering wheel for a moment, before sighing and pushing out of her car.

"I'm sorry," she began as the driver's door on the SUV opened. "I didn't see you—"

The rest of her words froze in her throat as tall, dark, and handsome got out.

He was the sexiest man she'd ever seen in her life, bar none. Towering at least a foot over her and with broad shoulders encased in tight black cotton, he had a thick black beard, piercing green eyes, and a smile that sucker-punched her right in the gut.

"There," she finished.

He lifted a brow, still smiling. "Obviously."

"I'm sorry," she said again. "I—"

He took a step toward her, those green eyes kind. "It's fine. It's just a car. Look, I—"

"It's not fine," she told him, waving her hands at the SUV. "Look at your car. Look what I *did!*" Unbidden, tears stung the backs of her eyes, and she blinked rapidly. It was an accident. She wouldn't cry. She couldn't cry over something she clearly hadn't meant to do. That would be absolutely ridiculous.

But this was the nail in the coffin on her emotions.

She was a jealous jerk, and single and lonely and alone— yes, she knew that lonely and alone were basically the same thing—but she supposed it was possible to be lonely while actually being around other people. And that also shouldn't be what she was thinking about right now. Not with tears threatening and not with the fact that she now needed to add shitty driver to her list of jealous, single, lonely, *and* alone.

A finger on her cheek, wiping away a tear that had escaped. "What's your name?"

"Misty Hansen," she whispered.

"Hi, Misty." He waited until she met his gaze. "I'm Chance —" His eyes broke away from hers. "Oh, shit." He shifted, running past her.

She turned to see what he was looking at.

Turned to see what he was too late to do anything about.

Her car—her freshly-paid off, awesome sedan was rolling forward . . . right into her brother's garage door.

*Crunch.*

Fuck. Her. Life.

"Jackson," he finished, looking back at her with wide green eyes.

---

Thank you for reading! I hope you loved meeting Soph and Rob as much as I loved writing them! The next book in the Life Sucks series is CLUSTERF*@K.

**She was single, almost pathetically so...and then the man ended up totaling her heart.**

CLICK HERE TO READ CLUSTERF*@K NOW>

And if you enjoyed DUMPSTER FIRE, you'll love the sexy, sweet, and close-knit Breakers Hockey crew. The first book in the series, BROKEN, is now live!

*"It is sexy, hot, adorable and such a fun read. You will not be able to put this down!"* —Amazon Reviewer

**I'd brought him home thinking that for once in my life I would live a little.** Now weeks later...I was puking my guts up and had a pink stick with a plus sign on it declaring my future.

DOWNLOAD BAD NIGHT STAND FOR FREE HERE >

I so appreciate your help in spreading the word about my books, including sharing with friends! Please leave a review on your favorite book site!

You can also join my Facebook group, the Fabinators, for exclusive giveaways and sneak peeks of future books.

If you'd like to receive emails from me for new releases and monthly giveaway sign up for my newsletter at https://www.elisefaber.com/newsletter

Want a free bonus story? Hate missing Elise's new releases?
Love contests, exclusive excerpts and giveaways?
Then signup for Elise's newsletter here!
https://www.elisefaber.com/newsletter

And join Elise's fan group, the Fabinators https://www.
facebook.com/groups/fabinators for insider information, sneak
peaks at new releases, and fun freebies! Hope to see you there!

LIFE SUCKS SERIES

Breakaway

Breakout

Checked

Coasting

Centered

Charging

Caged

Crashed

A Gold Christmas

Cycled

Caught

Cap

Covered

**_Breakers Hockey (all stand alone)_**

Broken

Boldly

Breathless

Ballsy

Bewitched

Blowout

**_Rush Hockey Trilogy_**

Big Puck Energy

Filthy Puckboy

So Pucking Over It

### *Love, Action, Camera (all stand alone)*

Dotted Line

Action Shot

Close-Up

End Scene

Meet Cute

### *Love After Midnight* (all stand alone)

Rum And Notes

Virgin Daiquiri

On The Rocks

Sex On The Seats

### *Life Sucks Series* (all stand alone)

Train Wreck

Hot Mess

Dumpster Fire

Clusterf*@k

FUBAR

Perfect Storm

Free Fallx

### *Roosevelt Ranch Series* (all stand alone, series complete)

Disaster at Roosevelt Ranch

Heartbreak at Roosevelt Ranch

Collision at Roosevelt Ranch

Regret at Roosevelt Ranch

Desire at Roosevelt Ranch

### *Phoenix Series* (read in order)

Phoenix Rising

Dark Phoenix

Phoenix Freed

### *Phoenix: LexTal Chronicles* (rereleasing soon, stand alone, Phoenix world)

From Ashes

In Flames

To Smoke

### *KTS Series (all stand alone, series complete)*

Riding The Edge

Crossing The Line

Leveling The Field

Scorching The Earth

### *Cocky Heroes World*

Tattooed Troublemaker

# ABOUT THE AUTHOR

*USA Today* bestselling author, Elise Faber, loves chocolate, Star Wars, Harry Potter, and hockey (the order depending on the day and how well her team -- the Sharks! -- are playing). She and her husband also play as much hockey as they can squeeze into their schedules, so much so that their typical date night is spent on the ice. Elise changes her hair color more often than some people change their socks, loves sparkly things, and is the mom to two exuberant boys. She lives in Northern California. Connect with her in her Facebook group, the Fabinators or find more information about her books at www.elisefaber.com.

facebook.com/elisefaberauthor

amazon.com/author/elisefaber

bookbub.com/profile/elise-faber

instagram.com/elisefaber

goodreads.com/elisefaber

pinterest.com/elisefaberwrite